SUMMARY

Book III in the Knights of the Board Room series

Nothing stands between a Master and the submissive he loves...

Peter Winston is K&A's operations manager and a National Guard captain. The night before he heads out on his second Afghanistan tour, he meets Dana, an Army sergeant and sexual submissive who gets into his head and heart the way no woman ever has.

Yet when they reunite one year later, life has drastically changed for Dana. With the sensual talents of the other K&A men, Peter sets the stage for another special night for them, knowing that only a submissive's willingness to trust her Master will bring her back to love and life again.

i

HONOR BOUND

A Knights of the Board Room Novella

JOEY W. HILL

Honor Bound

A Knights of the Board Room Novella - Book #3

Copyright © 2019 Joey W. Hill

ALL RIGHTS RESERVED

Cover design by W. Scott Hill

SWP Digital & Print Edition publication January 2019 by Story Witch Press, 452 Mattamushkeet Dr., Little River, South Carolina 29566, USA

Berkley Heat Digital & Print Edition publication February 2010 by the Penguin Group, 375 Hudson Street, New York, New York 10014, USA

The following material contains graphic sexual content meant for mature readers. Reader discretion is advised.

Digital ISBN: 978-1-942122-83-8

Print ISBN: 978-1-942122-87-6

ACKNOWLEDGMENTS

My sincere thanks to Phil and Kris. As a soldier who has done multiple tours in Iraq, Phil provided invaluable insight into the story details related to Peter and Dana's service in the military. Kris, his wife, was kind enough to let me pick Phil's brain right after his return home from an Iraq tour, which was incredibly generous. Any factual errors remaining are entirely my own.

I also want to thank wonderful fellow authors Kimberly Kaye Terry and Taige Crenshaw for reassuring me that a romance about two people who happen to be of different races *can* focus first and foremost on the love story. Ladies, if I screwed it up, that's also all on me!

CHAPTER ONE

"*I* can't believe you broke out the 1939 Macallan." Peter examined the bottle of whiskey. "You must think I'm going to die this time."

Ben slanted him a grin. "Well, it is your second tour. Two strikes."

"Man has that much luck, it's got to run out," Lucas agreed. The athletic CFO dodged Peter's affable punch, leaning back in the spacious VIP booth that allowed plenty of room for the five men, all at or above six feet tall, most of them with shoulder spans to match.

"You guys are terrible," their waitress decided, a dark-eyed Spanish beauty with a name tag that said *Maria*. With extreme pleasure, Peter noted the lushness of her breasts, presented with mouthwatering appeal over the tight hold of her velvet blue corset. Nothing got him going like a corset, the way it held a woman's body, the subtle implications of restraint. The guys knew him well. There was no better place than an upscale BDSM club to bring him the week before he shipped out.

"Honey, where you going?" she asked.

"Afghanistan."

"Iraq's too tame for him," Matt put in. "He'd be bored."

"He'll get slack, cozy up to some doe-eyed beauty with an IED under her burka. One a lot like you, gorgeous." Ben raised his empty glass, giving her a lazy, appreciative look.

She snorted delicately at the green-eyed, dark-haired lawyer and

1

flipped a corkscrew out of her short apron. "I better get a good tip from a group guzzling down Macallan. This goes for about ten grand, last I heard."

"Yeah, but he blew his entire wad on it," Jon said. "He's trying to compensate for spiritual emptiness with material goods."

Even as Jon spoke, Peter noted the engineering genius of their five-man team was gazing absently around the club, which probably meant Jon was solving physics equations, creating the next great invention, and meditating on the meaning of the universe, all while determining which woman he'd take to Nirvana with him tonight.

"Bullshit," Ben snorted. "You can be right with the universe *and* enjoy the finer parts of it. Like our gorgeous server. Want to share a sip with us, darling? There's room on Peter's lap, though you'll find far more to satisfy you on mine."

Peter kicked him under the table, but Maria laughed, expertly removing the cork. "Tempting, but not allowed, *precioso*. Do you like toffee?" she asked Peter.

As he nodded, she poured a draught and handed it to him. "Must be why your friend chose it. Despite his *mierda*, I think he knows a lot about you."

Ben raised a brow. "You've had Macallan before."

"You think you're the only high roller who's ever come through, *precioso*? This is The Zone, the most upscale fetish club in the South. And I do drink. When I'm off duty, and if the company's worthwhile." She gave him a saucy look, checking him out just as outrageously. "We're delighted to have you here. You call me if you need anything."

As she sauntered away in the skintight latex black pants, a diamond pendant dangling provocatively at her nape from the choker she wore, Ben leaned out. Peter gave Jon a nod and he shifted right, hard. Too late, Ben grabbed for the table, ending up on his ass on the floor as the men burst out laughing.

"All right, keep it up. Next time you guys get yourself in a legal snarl, this lawyer'll keep his mouth shut."

Matt Kensington, their boss, but as much a part of their group as the alpha wolf was part of the pack, bared his teeth in a grin. "You might not have a job for long."

"I know too much about all of you." Ben, unimpressed, put himself back in the booth with retaliation in his gaze. "Plus, no one else will put up with your crap. What do you think, soldier?"

Peter had taken a swallow. He closed his eyes. "Hell, Ben. This is the shit."

"I beg to differ. It is definitely not shit." But Ben smiled, poured for himself and the other three men. When they lifted glasses and brought them together, for a while nothing further was said, each contemplating the whiskey and why they'd brought Peter here.

None of them would talk about it tonight. Nothing serious, anyway, because Peter wouldn't want them to. They worked together in Baton Rouge as the management team of Kensington & Associates, the manufacturing acquisition company Matt Kensington had founded and made successful through their combined talents, but an unshakable bond existed between them whether they were around a boardroom table or a poker table.

There were a lot of things that went into that—shared experiences, ups and downs—but the fact that every one of them was an experienced sexual Dominant, preferring to use control and varying levels of pain to bring a woman mind-boggling pleasure, was the one that would hold the upper hand tonight.

That bond had only grown stronger when the dynamic changed. Lucas and Matt were both married now, but Peter wore a St. Christopher's medal that Matt's wife, Savannah, had given him for his last Afghanistan tour. He always wore it, like a favor from his monarch's queen. No one at the table would laugh at the thought. It didn't matter that they were hell and gone from those part-fantasy times of medieval chivalry—there was a code of behavior they exercised in business as well as personal life. A female columnist had picked up on it, coining them the Knights of the Boardroom. Or Soul-Sucking Predators of the Bayou, depending on who wrote it. Suppressing a smile, he glanced around the table.

Matt Kensington was every inch their leader, with his hawk features, dark piercing eyes and powerful build. Savannah, who was not present for this guys' night out, was a golden match for him, delicate as a princess but a tough-as-nails CEO herself, such that Matt had had to employ all their sensual talents to take her down and make her his. After he cut his heart out of his chest and offered it to her as a fair trade.

3

Lucas, K&A's CFO, was hell on wheels with numbers and identifying unprofitable acquisitions that could become moneymakers. He was also an amateur cyclist, which had stumbled him over Cassandra Moira on a cycling trip a year ago. He'd conducted her takeover as relentlessly as any Peter had seen him implement on their unfortunate targets, only his methods had been far more pleasurable and persuasive.

He envied both men their happiness, but was glad for them. Maybe the proximity of all that marital bliss was a contagious disease that couldn't help but make a man think about the possibility of permanence with a woman. But hell, you needed the right woman for that, and he believed in fate. He didn't worry about making it happen.

Jon would agree with that. He was the most spiritual of the crowd, into ancient history and philosophies, Tantra and meditation, despite their merciless male ribbing about stretchy shorts and yoga sessions. He would be amused to find Peter had such a Zen take on relationships, but there it was.

Recruiting a family wasn't in his immediate future, anyway, because being in the National Guard, seeking overseas assignments, was one of the ways he'd decided to give back. He didn't care if people thought it was old-fashioned or misguided honor bullshit. He liked bringing and enforcing the peace necessary for people to self-actualize. Having a front-row seat when and if they learned not to live in fear, seeing their kids play in the streets without being blown up... It made it all worthwhile.

He'd have time for a family or he wouldn't, but he was living the life he wanted to live. And Matt was more than supportive. Peter had no qualms about saying the men at this table were his family, Matt most of all. Peter's parents had died when he was in his teens. He'd had a rough time of it, but had entered the army young, done a three-year stint, and then, when he'd sought his degree, Matt had interned him at his burgeoning company, bringing a kid with blue-collar manufacturing aptitude and white-collar business systems understanding into this interior circle, an unconditional acceptance that he'd needed when the bottom fell out of his life.

Ah, hell. He hadn't drunk enough to be getting this sloppy sentimental. Shifting his thoughts, he focused on the prospect of comfortably slaking his lust on a willing submissive. As Ben made another

4

smartass comment and Jon came back with unruffled transcendental-ism, Peter lifted the Macallan to his lips with a smile.

～

Dana stood in the shadows to the right of the bar as Maria returned. When she glanced at the waitress, Maria gave her a smile, following the direction of her interest. "They're something, aren't they? Every one of them handsome as sin. Flew in from Louisiana to give their buddy a send-off. He's going to Afghanistan next week."

"The one at the end." Dana noted the military hairstyle, the way the dark blond man held himself upright, even as he enjoyed the male companionship.

"Appears so." Maria gave her a considering look. "They're all Doms, sweet. If you're looking for a hook-up, you could do a lot worse. They wouldn't be allowed in here if they weren't decent guys, but my impression is they're a cut above decent. The two on the inside are married. Wearing the rings and everything, and made it crystal clear they're just enjoying the view and here for their friend."

Dana nodded. The waitress's reassuring tone suggested she saw how nervous Dana was. But it was stupid, because she'd blown a wad of money on a temporary membership to The Zone for her two-week leave. She'd looked forward to this night for a while. It had been her decision to come alone. Not really the smartest idea, going to a new fetish club by yourself, but The Zone's rep was untarnished. Security inside and out, an intense vetting process that had taken the temp membership a couple months in advance to be approved, and she wore a slim bracelet that told staff she was new, so they'd keep an extra eye on her, help her know the ropes. Her lips curved. A good metaphor for a BDSM club. Her newness might be another reason Maria was giving her the pep talk.

She'd been a sexual submissive since her teens, but it had taken some mistakes and tears to figure it out. Once she did, she'd discov-ered the scene and never looked back. Though unfortunately, accepting and exploring her own sexual nature hadn't led to the imme-diate relief of frustration she'd hoped. It was a lot harder to find a compatible Dom worthy of her trust than she'd expected. Ironically, the same thing that made her crave a man's dominance was the same thing that made her keep them at arm's length. Most didn't put off the right vibe, or left her lukewarm. Subs at her club back home in Atlanta had told her it was like dating. You had to try on a few Doms, see what worked, what didn't. You couldn't keep holding out for the perfect one, the one that would take command of her senses from the very first second. You had to work at it.

So she'd tried harder, with fairly disastrous consequences. The Doms close to what she wanted were rife with those who could take it too far. Not because they were bad men, but because what she wanted was a lot like Goldilocks—rough, but not too rough. Her wants and needs were a moving target. She'd know it was right when it *felt* right. She couldn't describe it. She wanted to be completely taken over, but she resisted it at the same time. While she knew that was unreasonable, it didn't make it any less true.

Well, this was the freaking best fetish club ever, from what she'd heard. She had nothing to lose tonight. Because she'd chosen to come alone, no one knew her. What happened here would stay here, so she should stop skulking and do something, right? So—deep breath. She'd let her inhibitions go and...retreat while she still had a scrap of personal dignity.

C'mon, Dana. Get your shit together.

Her eyes went back to the soldier. When his hair grew out, did the sun lighten that wheat color? His eyes, thanks to the angle of the club lighting, showed storm-cloud gray, which might become steel, like the line of his jaw. He was on the end, probably not only because he was trained to be readily mobile, but because he had the widest shoulders and longest legs. Not one of her absolute requirements for a good Dom, but man, it sure added to the fantasy. The white shirt he wore with his jeans had to be tailored for those shoulders. As Maria had said, all of them reeked of money. And a man who sat like that had to be an officer. But she wasn't after the boy's cash. Just one night of his time. If she ever got up the courage to leave the corner.

"Are you having a good time?"

She started out of her mental struggle to find herself facing another tall and powerful man. He had dark, close-cropped hair and intense amber eyes that fairly screamed Dominant, causing a shiver to run over her skin. She could tell he noticed, but he remained smooth, professional. "I'm Tyler Winterman, one of the owners here. I wanted to make sure we were treating you right."

"Yes, sir." Only hours with a drill sergeant made Sergeant Dana Smith manage not to stutter the response. The "sir" was an instinctive deference to his status here that he seemed to take as his due, which everything about him said he should.

"Good." He ran a light, reassuring hand down her arm. "You look beautiful. A fortunate person should be very happy to meet you tonight. Would you like an introduction to someone?"

"I...um. Well, he might not...I don't know him." Her gaze flickered, a brief flash. Still, Tyler shifted and determined exactly whom she'd been looking at.

"Hmm. Why don't I leave it in his hands, then? You chose well, Dana. Let us know if you need anything."

He moved onward, leaving her gaping like a trout because he'd known her name. That surprise didn't keep her from noting he had a fine, fine walk. Slacks fitted right, shirt tucked in, thank you, Jesus. As a rep of the female gender, she was obligated to watch that tight ass, the predatory grace of a sex-on-Gucci-soles prowl.

Stopping at one booth, he stroked a proprietary hand over the moonlight-colored hair of a tall blue-eyed woman there. From the way her gaze warmed, whatever he said to her was obviously intimate. The amber eyes flamed in response. Giving a lock of her hair a tug, he moved away. Straight toward the table where Dana's blond soldier was sitting.

"Oh, no, don't. Don't you dare..." She stood, mesmerized, as he put a hand on her guy's shoulder, spoke low to him. If every man at that table turned around and stared at her, she was going to respond as if a grenade was hurled in her proximity. She'd dive behind the bar.

The blond stilled, glancing up at Tyler. Then he shifted his gaze right to her.

In those few milliseconds, Dana turned over thoughts of whether to meet his eyes, not meet his eyes. Smile, not smile. *Oh, crap.* This was what she always did. Worried about what she should or shouldn't do, when all she wanted was to be completely swept away, where no choices were hers, except the one where she needed to say good night at the end of the incredible experience and head back to her real life.

Even if she found her fucking romance novel, she had no delusions that it could be more than a one-night-only engagement.

This guy was perfect, because he had nothing in common with her —white, wealthy, likely an officer—but there was that irresistible vibe coming off of him. Drawing her like a bug to a zapper, which meant she might get disastrously burned. She wasn't complaining—*I promise, Grams*—but nothing in her life had been a fairy tale. Was it too much to ask for one solitary night that *was* like one?

She got her answer when his eyes locked with hers. While she knew she was standing by the bar, people moving past her, music vibrating the floor beneath her feet, dim light strobing, it all disappeared. She'd had that spark of sexual connection with Masters before. It was always thrilling, a toe-curling, delicious shot of anticipation. But this... Her breath went short, and she suddenly wanted nothing more than to be near him. It was scary as hell. And yet she stood stock-still, like some dumbass golden-haired princess, waiting to see if the prince would take command, bring her out of stasis into full, vibrant life.

"There's someone worth your attention at your two o'clock."

When Tyler Winterman, part-owner of The Zone, put his hand on Peter's shoulder, bent, and murmured that statement into his ear, Peter blinked. There'd been plenty of available women hovering since they arrived, and Ben had hinted they had someone special lined up for him. While Peter was down with that, he knew Tyler wouldn't draw his attention to just anyone. So he looked. And the second glass of Macallan he'd been lifting to his lips stopped halfway there.

Holy shit.

For a second, he thought he was looking at Ben's special arrangement, but because Ben knew Peter's tastes, he wouldn't have arranged for this girl. Not unless he'd reached ass deep inside of Peter and pulled out some unconscious dream he hadn't realized he had. All the attributes that Peter usually sought weren't obvious in this one. In fact, she wasn't *anything* like the women who usually attracted his attention. Yet here he was, unable to look away.

She was a black woman, for one thing. While the beauty of dark skin had teased his gaze before, he'd never felt pulled toward it as he did now. He had the taste of toffee on his tongue, making it easy to imagine her skin tasting like a complementary caramel, or a swirling chocolate. Or perhaps something spicy, exotic.

He liked his women tall and well endowed, with tits that he could fuck with his cock, lubricated with his pre-come. Or watch the curves move with generous abandon while he fucked her from behind, in front of a wide, well-lit mirror. This woman was petite, with an athlete's lean, hard muscle. The elegant slimness of her bearing made him wonder if there was Ethiopian in her background. She had a proud slope to her high forehead, the suggestion of sculpted cheek-bones and a precise chin, though the rest was hidden beneath a mask. When light strobed over her face, he saw the mask was deep purple and green with dangles of amethyst and emerald beads accentuating the delicate jaw.

A simple, short sheath covered her body, the black fabric translu-cent, fluttering as she breathed. Despite the fabric and dim light, he could tell her breasts were a small but pretty set, the curves likely a good fit for his hands. She wore a jeweled harness that included nipple clamps, such that he could imagine those stimulated peaks pressing into his palms. A chain ran between the clamps, down to a navel glit-tering with a temporary catch bead that hooked another delicate chain low on her hips, traveling around to the back. The scrap of dark thong made her look almost naked until he took a closer look, and lingered in that tempting shadowy area.

When he eventually raised his gaze, he took it to her neck. Many available subs wore a collar of some form, with an attached ring so that a Master might leash and claim them for the night, if both parties were willing. Hers was a high-neck ring collar, triple stacked, with a single steel diamond-shaped loop on it for the attachment.

As she waited, obviously knowing she was being evaluated, her eyes glittered behind the mask. Her lips parted. Slowly, she pivoted on one high heel. The five-inch stilettos made him bare his teeth in a feral smile at her clever attempt to add to her height. As she turned to face the wall, light shimmered across skin dusted with glitter powder. The sheath had an open back, draping down so he saw the delicate waist chain dropped a single teardrop pearl in the tender dimple of her tight, round ass. But it was what was tattooed across the small of her back, as precisely curved and sweet as a porcelain teapot, that got him to his feet. "Guys, I really appreciate the girl you got me, but there's been a change of plans."

As he moved across the room, he couldn't take his eyes from it. The boldness of the tat was too masculine for her feminine frame, but it showed well against her copper skin in the club's dim light. A twisted American flag, held in an eagle's talons, with a script beneath it.

Your freedom, my life. Armed services ink.

When he reached her, he stepped in close. He could say it was because the music was loud, but he wanted to be damn sure that signal was for him. Keeping her cheek pressed to the wall, she left her lashes lowered in that shy invitation. As he moved in, she shifted her legs apart. Offering to be evaluated further. Peter suppressed a growl.

She had short, close-cropped hair, and that high ring collar went from the base of her neck to the point of her skull. It limited her head's mobility, requiring an upright posture and dependence on a Master's direction. That, and the automatic spread of her toned, lean legs, which tilted up her delectable backside, confirmed she was an extreme player, firing his blood further.

Peter knew a woman gave up a piece of her soul every time she gave her body. Usually he let them decide how much of a piece to give, because his desires ran toward the more hardcore, the ones who had it deeper in their nature than just adding kink to their lives. But getting into the mind of a full-natured sub meant tapping into more-than-inside-the-club-walls fantasies. So he usually settled for a club-only sub, had a good time fantasizing about the possibility of more, and then went on his way.

Until this moment. For some reason, this slim creature made him think of what really fired his blood—a woman that was all his, for always. A woman whose submissive nature was a match for his Dominant one.

Drawing a steadying breath, he touched her nape, drifted down her spine toward that marking that had called to him, though he noted she had a couple other tattoos as well, shadowed by the sheath. Trembling under his touch, she made a quiet noise. He leaned in, pressing his thigh against her ass, the sensitive crease, his knee finding treasure between her parted thighs. Her breath caught.

With that closely shorn hair, he could see the shape of her ears. Delicate and perfect, like the rest of her. "So what's your rank, sweetheart?"

"Sergeant."

He'd meant it as a jest, assuming the tattoo to be a leftover from an ex-boyfriend. At least he hoped so, because he didn't mess with a woman who was still attached. But as he glanced over her again, he registered that the body he was looking at wasn't aerobically fit. It was combat fit. "Well, seeing as I'm a captain, I outrank you."

A smile teased her soft, full mouth, so moist from a burgundy lip gloss it made him think of an entirely different set of lips. "Yes, sir," she murmured.

Unable to resist and wanting to test, he didn't ask. He slid a hand between her spread legs. Soaking wet against the panel of those nearly nonexistent thong panties. She let out a harsh gasp, and his eyes sharpened. "Not used to a man just taking you over, are you? But that's what you crave."

She closed her eyes, biting her lip. Nodded, and his blood went to full boil.

"I want you tonight." He usually had more finesse, but he made it a rough demand, no question, request or games. The urgency that gripped him now had nothing to do with the limits of time. "I want that collar and those jewels off. They're not mine."

When she removed them, taking a breath at the tug to the nipple clamps, she laid them on the bar for an efficient Maria to tag and place beneath it. Then she lifted her chin. Peter slid his fingers over the fragile network of arteries pumping at an accelerated rate and tightened slightly, creating a collar of flesh and bone. Her pulse elevated. "Better. Look at me."

She did, and he was caught by that gaze, a pale green like summer grass, quiet lagoons and women's springtime lawn dresses. Overwhelmed by dark, hungry pupils.

"Give me your hands." He took out the short tether he'd been given as a guest Dom at the club and unwound it.

She held them out, but as he looped the tether around her wrists, the slim fingers found him under his untucked shirt, hooked in the waistband of his jeans, knuckles brushing his abdomen intimately.

His lips twisted. "Interpreted that order in your own way, didn't you? That'll earn you some disciplinary action."

When her eyes sparked, he knotted the tether to bind her to him. She kept her fingers where they were, and his aching cock was already chafing, straining toward that touch. Maybe she felt his heat, but her rising desire was as palpable as his own. He wasn't going to take her back by his table, but straight to a room where he could see how much of a fight she liked. If her need to make a man work to be her Master matched his desire to prove he could acquire that target, it was going to be a hell of an experience.

"Is this a first time for you, sweetheart?"

Her voice was throaty, velvet sin. "I sure hope so."

CHAPTER TWO

*T*he advantage to two strangers hooking up in a BDSM club, versus in a bar, was there wasn't a lot of awkward small talk, the need to get to know each other. One led, one followed, the basic rules established, and the game began. Dana preferred that, though it was yet another ludicrous paradox about what she wanted. It was impossible to achieve the emotional rapport she wanted with a Master that way.

So she'd thought.

This one was keeping her off balance. He'd brought her to a private playroom, but not a dungeon, a Victorian drawing room or a stable, some of the more hardcore settings. It was an honest-to-God garden, with plants and sod, and lights that could be darkened to show a holographic heavy moon and glittering stars above.

If she didn't know for sure they were still within The Zone, she would have thought he'd taken her outside. The silver light reflected on her skin like moonlight in truth. Gleaming in that same light was a statue of Aphrodite, and a fountain with prancing unicorn sculptures around it. No whips, chains or restraints that she could see. While she was impressed with the production, the exorbitant temporary member fee worth every dime for props alone, it seemed like a soft setting. She liked it hard. Had she chosen wrong? It wasn't the first time she'd had to steer a new Master in the right direction.

She lowered her voice to a practiced persuasive purr. "Perhaps my

Master thinks his new slave can't handle it rough and dark. Perhaps he'd like to ask her the types of things she's willing to do for him."

Her Master-for-the-night turned. The storm-cloud eyes were dark in the dim light, but the moonlight sculpted the planes of his face, giving him an implacable look of irresistibly cruel sensuality, vibrating life and power.

"Take off your shoes."

Most Masters wanted the stilettos to remain on, and she liked it that way, too. When you were five foot nothing, the shoes gave that sense of stature, the fuck-me sway of the hips and elongated calves that drew a man's gaze. Without them, she felt a little too close to the "short scrapper" she'd been dubbed as a kid, because of the day she'd beaten up two boys on the corner who'd tried to take Robbie's lunch money. It had taken Robbie a couple years to forgive her for that. But now he was dead, and forgiveness was out of her hands.

Damn, two seconds with the guy and she was already tapping family shit? She needed to take control of this, get out of this environment and into one where she was more comfortable.

She kicked off the shoes, but before she could draw a breath, he stepped forward and scooped her up with graceful, easy power. His hands were big and warm on her thighs and back. His hard abdomen muscles flexed as he walked, body shifting under the point of her hip. Taking her to the fountain, he studied it and then sat her down on the edge, letting her feet curl into the thick grass. The fountain wall was embedded with smooth stones like goose eggs, pressing intimately into the valley between her thighs, the seam of her buttocks. A fragrance in the water's mist teased her nose. Behind the rush of the water, she could hear crickets and frogs.

"You'll speak only when spoken to," he said with deceptive mildness. "And your safe word is 'freedom.' Don't move from where I've placed you." As he released her, he passed his fingers along the eagle tattoo, grazing the dress's low back, making her shiver. Despite her doubts, she thought "freedom" might be the last word she said to him.

Straightening, he propped a foot on the wall. His leg flanked her, his body dwarfing her with his sheer size. As he undid the cuffs of his shirt, he examined her, slow and easy. When he began to unbutton it down the front, her mouth went dry, but she didn't get the feeling he was performing for her. Everything about his body language said *she* was the center-stage show, there to serve as his entertainment. As he took his time, her lower belly was drawing tighter, an odd quake in her thighs because she didn't know what he planned. Even if she was the woman regularly in his bed, she thought she still wouldn't know with a man like this. He'd keep the control, and he'd keep her guessing.

The moonlight caught the silver of his dog tags, as well as a St. Christopher's medallion that fell above them. It captivated her, seeing her Master's personal things. *Winston, Peter R.* That was his name.

Wanting to break the strange feeling knowing his name evoked, as well as the sense of helplessness he'd imposed on her, she reached out to help him unbutton the last two buttons of his shirt. As her fingertips grazed the cotton, her lips parted, tongue touching them in anticipation.

In one swift movement, he captured her hands in one of his, pushed them down so they were cupped between her legs. The contact, her own hands against her pussy, the pressure of his hand against them, arched her up. Her head fell naturally into the cup of his other palm as he brought his mouth onto hers.

Men kissed all different ways, and she'd sampled quite a few of them. Despite that, she had no way of classifying this one. It was a command in a kiss. He didn't ask to take over; he just did, as if he knew he could take anything he wanted from her. Whether she said yes or no was irrelevant to him. He'd brought her into this kind of setting for a reason. *He* was the hardcore trappings, the dungeon, the spanking bench and whips. If he'd taken her into a dungeon, she might have been terrified down to her toes. She probably still was, but the setting helped balance what he was putting her through now, kept the danger to a thrilling edge, on the near side of the teetering plunge where she'd lose her mind.

His tongue went deep, exploring teeth and moist flesh, the roof of her mouth and all the hot crevices in a flexible, stroking way that said he was quite aware of which part of a woman's body was most closely related to her mouth. As he rocked her backward, he released his hold on her hands. She would have grabbed on to his biceps for support, but something told her to keep her hands where they were, and she was smart enough not to move them against herself without his permission. But it was difficult.

When gravity took her down farther, he moved right with her, his arm locked securely on her lower back, fingers spread to hold her buttock tight. As he held her over the fountain's gurgling waters, the aromatic mist touched her skin. She wanted to touch his corded throat and short hair. While the shirt wasn't open all the way, the muscled and broad expanse she'd glimpsed had a scattering of fine gold hair dusted across it.

He increased his grip on her buttock, making her mewl. She gasped into his mouth as his thigh insinuated itself between her legs, pressed against her wet heat. It also pushed her back farther, so her ass was hanging over the edge of that wall. He pulled up the bottom of her sheath dress, catching the thin ribbon of her thong in his clever fingers. He moved both out of the way an instant before two well-placed jets of water surged up from the fountain pool, hitting her clit and anus with insistent pressure. The water was cool enough to be a shock, warm enough to make her squirm against it, creating friction. Now she understood why he'd placed her exactly where he had.

"Be still," he warned her, those eyes close, the mouth gone from sensual to stern and uncompromising. Though he hadn't touched her mask, it felt stripped away, his gaze boring into hers. "You going to keep trying to run things, Sergeant?"

A girl from her usual club had told her there were two types of Dominants: the mechanical and the psychological. *The good ones mix it, you know. The setting, the toys, the mind games. But the really psychological Doms, they're rare. I've met one or two, and girl, they're the scariest and most tempting of all. They seem like they know everything about you from the get-go, and they don't need to do a single thing to have you licking their boots.*

She wasn't sure she was into boot licking, but that wasn't what her girlfriend had meant anyhow. It meant something way more than that. She had a feeling she was confronting it at close-quarters distance. Actually, make that point-blank.

He'd told her to be still, but those water jets made it impossible. Her body had to jitter and squirm in response. "I'm sorry, sir," she gasped. "I can't."

"Like I thought. A discipline problem." He lifted her away from the jets and, with that same effortless strength, flipped her over. Now he was sitting on the wall and she was on his lap, her wet, glistening bottom perched high. She couldn't help herself. She gripped the tough denim over his calf and put her mouth on him, biting into the fabric.

16

God, he smelled edible. A man with money and good grooming knew how to seduce a woman's nose with the right aftershave and soap, keeping the earthy scent of male as the perfect complement to the mix.

"Five feet and a hundred pounds of trouble."

A hundred fifteen, but who was arguing? Most of that fifteen was in her ass and tits. No man Dana knew had ever complained about that.

"Lift your arms straight out in front of you."

Not an easy feat when you were folded over a man's thighs, but she locked her stomach muscles and that shapely ass to comply, and earned a noticeable twitch from the iron bar of his cock, pressed hard against her belly as an incentive. Blessing every agonizing workout where she'd pushed herself on strength training, she threw in a not-so-subtle rub against him.

He smacked her ass, and it wasn't some passing swat. Holy God, the man had some power behind that arm. The wobble of her buttock in response rocked up her spine. "You're going to piss me off, little girl, and that's not something you want to do. You haven't chosen a Master who can be led around by his cock tonight."

Uncertainty and indignation flooded her. She didn't do that. She was looking for a Master who would take the reins. It wasn't her fault most of them didn't.

He reached down, making her realize there were compartments in the fountain wall. Because of her position, she couldn't see, but after the sound of a hydraulic door closing, he straightened. While she suspected he could hold her with perfect balance, he shifted so she rocked, caught off guard, and had to grab at him again.

"Arms out, soldier," he barked, and gave her a matching handprint on the opposite cheek.

"I was falling, sir."

He put his hand on the back of her neck, exerting enough pressure that she had to strain to keep her upper body up and arms out as he'd demanded. This was bringing back some harrowing memories of Basic Combat Training. But Basic was about breaking the person down, remaking and retraining them, wasn't it? She swallowed.

Leaning down so his breath was against her ear, he had that implacable hand suddenly caress her nape in a way that sent nerves yearning toward his touch. "If you're falling, trust me to catch you, Sergeant."

Before she could respond to that, he'd straightened and clasped her wrists. He'd retrieved gauntlets with lacings, so he could tie her arms together, wrists to elbows. As he worked the fabric down over her forearms and then began to thread and draw the lacings tight, her stomach and ass muscles quivered. The lifted position was becoming excruciating. But he'd ordered her to do it, and damn it, she'd do it.

His dog tags plinked against her back. The cool metal against her flesh was in contrast to the burning in her stomach and shoulder muscles, the ache in her neck. He was taking his damn time, even though he never faltered, weaving those two gauntlets with smooth precision. Every time he pulled a section taut, the increased restraint coiled up the need in her pussy the same way.

"You like that, don't you? What would you think of a full corset, one of those cruel hourglass makers that robs you of breath and puts your pretty tits on high display, drawing a Master's gaze to your accessible ass?"

She shuddered, thinking of how deliciously restrictive it would be. How did he know she'd fantasized about that? She had a couple, but Masters had unlaced her out of them, never into them. Not as if she was their possession, a gift they prepared for themselves. When she'd fantasized about it, she'd also fantasized about a Master like this one appeared to be.

"Yeah, you like that idea, I can tell. I like a corset on my slave. It shows off how beautiful she is, all those womanly curves, the boning keeping her straight and proud, knowing she's got nothing to worry about. Because she's mine."

She closed her eyes, lost in the pleasure of the thought. She wasn't a woman who sought the shelter of a man, but for some reason the idea of being his like that gave her a welcome sense of sanctuary, a place she could count on when she needed it. It was a dangerous thought, because loneliness, dwelling on the fact she had no family left, could too often take her down the wrong road.

The leftover lacing was wrapped over the hand he put beneath her curled fingers, as though he were offering a branch to a bird. "Rest your weight now."

She wanted to hold out longer to prove she could, but her

straining body overrode her, her gasping muscles letting out a cry of relief. Then the movement of his body told her he'd pulled his dog tags over his head. He broke the latch, wrapped the chain around her neck twice and snapped it shut again one-handed, an impressive feat. The beaded chain tightened on her throat when he cupped her chin, stroked his thumb along the corner of her mouth to get her to open up, and then slid the tags onto her tongue.

"Close your teeth on them."

She did, so the edge of one was visible between her lips, the chain swinging against her chin. He stroked her back. "Good girl. You drop them, and I'll be very displeased. You think this is a cushy environment, don't you? No dungeon, no clever, cruel metal devices made to torture flesh. It's too soft. Isn't that right, Sergeant?"

His voice had that dangerous purr to it again, so she nodded her head, a quick jerk. She didn't even think about lying.

"You know your Bible? 'And out of the ground made the Lord God to grow every tree that is pleasant to the sight...'"

She did know her Bible, but was surprised that he would use it here. Her curiosity about that was short-lived, however. Apparently those compartments held more than man-made items. He brought a thin, whiplike branch into her line of sight. Not a polished switch, lacquered and placed for sale in The Zone's diverse gift shop. This was one that had been cut and peeled, much as someone might have done in ages past to take a child behind the woodshed. Or an errant wife, in the days of the "one-inch thick" rule.

Holy God, switches hurt. She didn't know if she could...

He was sliding it along her buttocks. "I'm going to teach you that when I give you an order, you follow it, Sergeant. I don't care how hot you are, how wet your cunt. What you want to happen or you're nervous about. I'm your Master and you trust and obey everything I tell you, to the letter. When I tell you not to move, you don't move. When I tell you to move, you move your ass as if it's on fire." The tip teased her pussy and she wiggled before she thought, then froze, but it was too late.

"Fire it is."

He brought down the switch. *Holy Jesus—Gram, forgive me.* Three successive strikes and she was yelping against those metal tags, feeling the edges against her tongue, but she wouldn't let them go. She'd learned her lesson. He'd given them to her; she was going to hold on to them.

He ran his hand over her smarting ass. She was shaking. God, when was the last time she'd shaken like a newbie during a session?

"You want your freedom, Sergeant?"

She was blowing like a winded horse around the outsides of those tags, saliva escaping in a mortifying display. But she shook her head. Tears she didn't understand clogged her throat.

"There you are, baby," he murmured. "That's the sub in you, rising to the top like cream. Like this kind of cream." His fingers passed through the honey of her pussy. "You just needed some focus. Got to get your mind on your proper business." He traced the eagle tattoo again, following the ripple of the gathered flag; then he made a wide loop to cruise up her back. She had two other tats, not as visible through the sheath's mesh, because they were simple pen and inks. He was resting on one now: the Lord's Hands. Dog tags were inked in a wrap around them, inscribed with *In God We Trust*.

Doms usually stayed away from that one. Too spiritual or personal, and the clubs weren't a place for strangers to get close in that kind of way. Only for pain and pleasure, and losing yourself in a place far beyond the mundane.

"Looks like you made a promise to your grandmother." His touch descended to the script below it. *I'll never forget, Gram.* "No matter what shit you see, you told her you'd keep Jesus and His teachings in mind. Let Him help you with every hard decision a soldier has to make. I like that."

Breath shuddered through her lungs as he moved to her final tattoo, a rendering of Athena. "This one's all for you, though. You call on her to forget the fear, give you a warrior's courage. Mixing the Christian and pagan together, because a soldier needs tactical support wherever she can get it. The devil never lacks for representation out in the field."

What was he doing to her? Slow, sensuous circles on her stung buttocks, words that were stripping away shields most Doms never touched. But she'd known, hadn't she? He didn't need the dungeon. This was what he did to a woman. He flayed away the skin, left her completely exposed. Was this what she'd signed up for?

Apparently so. Because, despite the fear and uncertainty, "free-

dom" had never felt more unappealing to her. Her fingers closed infin-
itesimally where they were hooked over his. So slight, it might be
taken for a simple involuntary twitch of her body. She cursed herself
for a coward. She had that Athena tat for a reason. Closing her eyes,
she tightened her grip, passed her fingers back and forth over his
knuckles. If she was being the sub she was used to being, she'd
provoke him with a grip suggesting what those fingers would do if
they were on his cock. Instead, she moved in a tender caress on his
curved fingers, tracing the calluses, the tough male skin.

"Oh, sweetheart, you're a treasure. You don't even realize it, which
makes me harder." He turned her, lifting her in the cradle of his arms
again, and stepped right into the fountain, unconcerned about his
jeans or the scuffed-looking cowboy boots he wore under them.

He took her to the Aphrodite, which Dana realized was not sinu-
ously posed without purpose. Peter set her down against the statue, so
her bottom rested on the goddess's bent knee. Stretching her arms up
and back, he laced the extra gauntlet ties to a discreet ring embedded
at Aphrodite's throat, part of her jewelry. The alabaster folds of her
artful dress formed hard curves through which he threaded Dana's
feet, pointing her toes with fingers caressing her arches and the sensitive ankles. When he stepped back, gravity and resistance kept Dana
firmly restrained. Aphrodite's ample cleavage pressed into her back so
her own breasts jutted out.

When his hands closed on her there, she could tell in his absorp-
tion and touch that her captain was an avid breast man, making her
wish she had more to offer him there. But he was so thorough,
exploring the way they molded into his palms, testing their weight,
tugging the nipple clamps and staring at her stimulated nipples in a
way that had them aching. It left her feeling as though they were more
than enough for him.

"My favorite thing," he murmured. "Suckling pretty tits until I
make you come. But there are some other things we need to handle
first."

He shrugged his shirt off his shoulders, his gaze drifting up to her
mouth, the way she continued to hold his tags. But when he turned to
toss the shirt over the fountain wall, letting it flutter to the grass, she
drank him in greedily, glad he wasn't a Dom who required her to lower
her eyes. One set of biceps bore the *Don't Tread on Me* flag with its

coiled serpent. Celtic styled letters formed an arch over the massive breadth of his shoulders. *PEACE.*

She understood why he'd put it there, because it had the same meaning the Lord's Hands did to her. They fought to protect and preserve, but any soldier who'd seen the carnage of war yearned for the day when love would prevail. And hoped there'd be some recognizable vestige of himself left when it finally arrived.

The soul of this man was strong, strong enough to surround her and carry her through anything. The unexpected thought startled her. She'd heard things like that from subs who'd been broken down to the point their most vulnerable needs and truths were revealed. She hadn't thought she was there, but her heart was telling her something different. He'd barely touched her physically, but she already felt owned by him, through and through.

He hadn't moved, holding her gaze as if he knew something intense was going on with her. Maybe for him as well. Reaching out, he traced her mouth, taking away the embarrassing saliva with a knuckle. There was a softness in his gray eyes, something that made the coil in her lower belly pull in two directions, toward her heart as much as the throbbing need between her legs.

Please do something. Hurt me. Fuck me. I don't care. Just don't strip me like this so fast. She should spit out the tags, take whatever punishment he could dish out. Anything but this freakish scenario straight from a romance novel, offering love at first sight and everything that went with that improbable scenario.

Yeah, in the middle of a BDSM club with your legs spread and your tits thrust out. Get a grip, Dana. Had she deluded herself to make her fantasy a reality?

He'd picked up a small remote from an alcove to the right of the statue. When he pressed it, water started flowing off the branches of the palm tree draping over Aphrodite's head. It poured down, filtering under her eye mask so Dana had to turn her face into Aphrodite's cheek. The water spread out, taking a dozen different routes along her throat and over her curves. That flood, as well as the fragrant mist rising, soaked through the thin fabric of her sheath, pasting it to her body.

On the bottom of the pool was an artful three-dimensional scroll design, but when he bent in an attractive ripple of muscle, a pull of denim at groin and thigh, she saw through her wet lashes that not all of them were decoration. Some were long, thin hoses. He straightened one, and the pinpoint nozzle on the end warned her ahead of time. Her clit spasmed in remembrance, her already moist pussy beginning to prepare for him anew.

"If you come without my permission, I'll give you ten more lashes with that switch," he said. "You keep a Master at arm's length, suck his dick and let him paddle your cute butt, call you a naughty girl. You think you're a badass. But on the inside you're a total pussy, sweetheart."

Her reaction wasn't calculated. She snarled and almost dropped the tags, showing her teeth. He showed her his in return, a devastating smile, but there was a heat in his eyes, a hardness to his jaw that told her the intensity wasn't all one-sided.

"You want way more than that. That's why those tags are in your mouth. Remember who you belong to."

The words were a somersault, from outright combat to lovemaking. Helpless here, tied and spread before him, that water licking down her body, she knew the pasted sheath highlighted every crevice and curve, the jut of her nipples. He hadn't taken anything off her but her shoes, and she'd never felt so naked. He hadn't taken off the mask because he didn't need to do so. He was laughing at her attempts to mask who and what she was.

He started at her nipples, playing with them like a cold, forked tongue, making her gasp with need, then washed the water over the high curve, hitting the crease beneath. Her body undulated, breasts quivering for him. Then he dropped and the water jet hit her clit dead on, shuddering through her body like voltage. No, no, no...

Oh, God. From the first second, she lost. No matter how much she wanted to do so, she couldn't control her body's reaction, because he was flicking his fingers through the spray, idle movements changing the friction. She bucked against the hold of the restraints, her ass slapping hard against Aphrodite's unrelenting knee. She bit down on the metal, felt the raised type of his name and rank, who he was. Her Master.

She wouldn't whimper, wouldn't plead. Son of a bitch thought he could get under her skin, into her head. She didn't want that. She wanted... God, she didn't know what the hell she wanted. She couldn't think, immersed in sheer, tsunami-powered feeling.

She wanted to lose. It would give him pleasure to switch her ass. That was what he wanted. He was her Master. She wanted to do whatever made him hard, whatever would make him want only her. But in the end, it didn't matter what she wanted. He already knew, and he took away all choices. The orgasm hit her like a tidal wave, so intense it was painful. Though her clit was over-sensitized, she wasn't in a position to move away from the stimulation. She screamed and screamed and screamed, the only thing left in her tumbling mind the need to keep a pit-bull grip on those tags, though more saliva pooled, slipping out around them. Fortunately the water washed it away, while the orgasm took everything else.

As she slowly descended to occasional, spasmodic jerks, she was mumbling around the tags, trying to clear the water from her eyes, her body shaking so hard. She needed his arms, his body, his heat. *Please, Master. Master.* That was what she was mumbling, though it registered only in a far-distant part of her floating head.

When he came to her, bringing the hard heat of his bare chest against her, tears spilled out without reservation this time. Locking his hands over her laced wrists, he pressed his mouth to her cheek below the mask. Though the water continued to flow over them, over her face, she was sure he knew she was crying.

He pulled back, but she kept her eyes closed, unsure if she could handle whatever he had planned next. She couldn't hear anything over the rush of water, and her body was vibrating so violently it provided its own low roar in her mind, clouding everything else.

When he returned to her, she moaned against the tags. He was blissfully naked, his knees against her thighs as he leaned into her, taking hold of her wrists again and bringing that fine chest closer to her face, so she could press into it, wishing she could open her mouth, taste water and heat.

His cock pressed between her legs, the head finding her with unerring accuracy. She was so slick and wet, she sucked him in like her mouth, but Jesus, he was a big man all over. She couldn't raise her legs, couldn't control anything as he pushed into her, slow and inexorable, refusing to be denied, no matter the tightness of her entry in this position. With the water running over her face, her sight and hearing were limited. But that made every sensation more excruciatingly noticeable. The shape of his broad head, the hard but delicious malleability of his cock, learning the unique feminine shape of her channel. He'd used a condom, since the club allowed nothing less, but she wondered what bareback would have felt like with this much heat and hardness. Her hold on the tags had increased to the point the chain had constricted on her neck, biting in, a collar he'd created only for her.

She wanted to hold on to his taut ass as he pounded into her, feel the flex of it. His thighs pressed to the insides of hers, his sheer size widening her, despite the ankle restraints. Her body was still going, moving with every movement of his, her aftershocks as strong as some orgasms she'd had with other lovers.

Please, please come. She begged him in her mind. She wanted to give him that release, give him anything. He was gorgeous, strong, everything she desired. Totally merciless and totally protective, all at once. She didn't know how to explain that thought, but it was in everything he was doing.

Tilting up as much as she could to give him even more access, she stroked his cock with her inner muscles to tell him how she felt. His fingers bruised where they gripped her wrists, and yet she saw his gaze flicker over her face with infinite desire and something deeper as she risked a look. She'd relish every mark he left on her, trace the dark smudges for days afterward.

"You want me to come, baby?"

She nodded, fast, quick, spoke the garbled words against water and metal. "Please, Master."

"Squeeze me harder with that sweet cunt. Tell me how much you want it."

She put everything she had into it, despite the fact she felt weak as a newborn kitten. However, it was enough. He leaned in, seized her mouth again. It was exquisite torture, the tip of his tongue on the seam of her closed lips, licking at her the way he might lick at her pussy, teasing those lips into full, puffy arousal.

She squeezed harder than she ever had, and started working herself as much as her bonds allowed, stroking, moving faster, though her lungs fought for air and her body strained at the limits of exhaustion. She'd give him everything; she just wanted him to...

With a deep, guttural noise, total male animal in rut, he let go. His face stretched into that sexy rictus of pleasure, lips drawing back from strong teeth, nostrils flared and eyes glazing and yet firing at once, the brow drawing down to emphasize the fierceness of his response. She reveled in it, her body trying to keep up, but she had no reservoir left. She sank down on him, grunting at every powerful thrust, telling him she wanted more, more, more. He'd left her lips, her nose, pressing into the hollow of his throat, burrowing, as he used her body for his release.

When at last he slowed, he brought her face up for a lingering tease of her lips again, his eyes open and holding hers as he did it. He kept doing it until a slow liquid heat began to unfurl in her. She didn't think it possible, but she was unable to control her reaction. A true Dom, he knew when he had her juices re-surging, because he slid back from her then, releasing the restraints that held her to the statue.

This time she didn't try to catch herself or control her descent, and she sagged into his waiting arms. When he carried her out of the fountain, plush towels already laid out on the sod made her wonder what Zone employee had seen her being pleasured. Had that enviable employee seen him ramming into her, that magnificent ass flexing?

As he laid her down on the towels, he continued to treat her as if she was his in all ways. He positioned her arms over her head and then, with one casual jerk, he ripped the thin dress she wore. Spreading it out to either side, he tenderly removed the nipple clamps, even though the blood rushed back to them painfully. He knew, for he bent and closed a warm, soothing mouth over one, making her whimper again, everything in her weak and out of control. He took his time about it, slow, methodical licks of his tongue, soft suckling, then moved to the other until she couldn't help but move restlessly beneath him.

All barriers to her body gone, he picked up a towel from the additional stack next to him and began to massage terry cloth over her skin, making her whimper when he ran it across her breasts, her breath sucking in at the sensitivity of the area.

Then he reached her pussy and her legs loosened automatically for him, earning an approving nod. Setting the towel aside at last, he leaned down, used his mouth to clasp the chain, slowly draw the tags from her lips. For a moment she held on to them, locking her jaw. His brow rose, a glint coming to his gaze. When at last she released them, he removed them, his fingers caressing, and returned the tags to his neck. She saw she'd left tooth marks, and was thrilled that he'd carry a reminder of her.

Since she was already there, it was a natural desire to look even lower, but she hesitated, looked back up at him.

"Look your fill, sweetheart." He put his thumb to the corner of her mouth. "You didn't cut yourself, did you?"

She shook her head, and looked. Down that powerful chest, to the sectioned abs, the conditioned body of a trained soldier. His cock was impressive even in semi-resting state, lying on the corded thigh muscles. She saw scarring in the abdomen area, though, scarring she recognized. A bullet injury, as well as some strikes that could have come from narrow brushes with explosions.

"Afghanistan," he provided. "I'm pleased to see you aren't marked that way."

"Yet," she whispered.

Gray clouds could become steel in an instant, she realized, as he leaned close again, his heated breath on her face. It made her lips yearn to taste, even as she trembled at what was in his face. Something no man had ever shown her with such undeniable clarity. Possessiveness.

"You'll keep your head and this fine ass down, Sergeant, so it stays that way. And I haven't forgotten those ten switch strikes. I'll make sure I send you off with a reminder to obey me in that."

She swallowed, fearing and anticipating that switching, curling her fingers into the sod above her head, even as her pussy moistened further. He went to one hip next to her, propping his head on his fist, and stroked his fingers over her clit, watching her reaction. "Tell me your name. Your real name."

CHAPTER THREE

*D*ana Esther Smith. Her voice had been soft but strong, like the flow of a river current he could feel on all his extremities, and perhaps even deeper than that.

Hours later, he'd escorted her back past his table, headed for the locker area. Matt and Lucas had been holding the fort. Matt had raised his glass, giving him his blessing. If Ben had still been there, he knew the lawyer's eyes would have lingered a little too long on Dana's tempting backside. That was Ben, always trying to get something started. Hell, he and Ben had shared a willing submissive before. But this time the thought raised his hackles, made him glad Ben was otherwise occupied.

The whole night had been full of unexpected surprises. He normally preferred a woman with no ink, but the three she had were such tantalizing clues into her head. Despite a jaded, sophisticated world, they suggested she was up-front about her gut convictions, like him. But emotionally there was shielding, complexity. It was what made a woman so damn appealing and frustrating at once.

He'd done what he'd promised, switched her pretty butt good, though a part of him didn't want to mark that delectable flesh with such angry red stripes. While he'd wanted to play more with her sweet tits, his focus had been getting past those shields. Afterward, he'd made her kneel, take him in her mouth, a true submissive's favorite posture, and had her suck him back to life with that skillful, devil-blessed mouth. She'd tried to sass him a couple times when the feelings they conjured in that magical room overcame her. He'd taken care of that. Repeatedly. But he couldn't claim to be any less shaken up. With Dana, he'd not only wanted more; he'd taken it, forced her to that brink with him.

She came toward him now, because they'd agreed to meet at the entrance before she took off. She'd changed into jeans and a snug black tee. The little tease had left off a bra, probably realizing he couldn't keep his eyes off a woman's breasts. The jut of her nipples and wobble of her small curves were damn distracting, but he didn't miss that she was trying to play it cool. She'd left the purple and green mask on. Giving him a friendly but distant smile, she went to her toes and brushed his mouth with hers. "It was a great night, Captain. A once-in-a-lifetime, God's truth."

Astonishingly, she was pulling away, intending to head for one of the waiting taxis. He caught her wrist, yanked her back to him. Pushing her up against the wall, he treated himself to a rough squeezing of those curves while he kissed her hard and deep, no passing brush of lips. When he lifted his head, her eyes were glazed behind the mask, her lips parted and heart beating fast.

"Trying to play me again, Sergeant?"

She swallowed, shook her head, but he was satisfied to see he'd broken that calm exterior. "I just... I can't give you more than tonight, Captain. I want to, but I've got to keep my head on straight. I'm only on leave. Maybe another time, another place... I won't be back for a year."

Fuck, what was he doing? He was leaving for Afghanistan next week himself. How could he demand more? Because there was a hell of a lot more there, and no man in his right mind turned his back on that much treasure. He forced himself to look past his own feelings and at her stiff body language, registering the thready pulse. It didn't matter if she was knocked off her axis, too; Dana obviously hadn't intended to take her Zone experience any further than this. When a woman got spooked, she needed her space, time to think. He couldn't push her now, no matter how much he wanted to. The problem was, by the time she thought it through, he'd be on a plane, and she'd be God knew where.

Damn it, earlier he'd calmly accepted fate's direction for his future relationships. If fate was true, he'd see her again. Right? Tonight, he had to let it go.

Releasing her reluctantly, his hands lingering, he nodded. Fought back something that made no sense, that told him to fuck fate, to keep her here with him. Always. "Take care of yourself, Sergeant."

She hesitated, maybe because she felt that resistance from him, or maybe because he was crazy enough to think she felt it from herself. Then she nodded, her fingertips grazing his forearm. Her breasts moved in that quivering, sexy rhythm as she moved to the cab. When he held the door for her, he noticed the slender nape of her neck still bore the faint imprint of his dog tag chain. After he shut the door, she put her hand up to the glass. He tried to meet her palm to palm, but then the cab pulled into traffic and his fingers slipped off. At last glimpse, he could tell she was taking off her mask, a shadow disappearing into the night.

It took a full five minutes of staring into the empty street, his mind circling itself, before he shook himself out of it, turned and went back to the club.

For the next hour and one additional bottle of Macallan, he managed to convince himself he'd done what he should. He responded automatically to Matt and Lucas, shutting out their curious glances. Sure, fate would bring them back together. That and electronics. She was in the military; he was in the military. He could find her. But a year was a fucking long time. He'd left it pretty open-ended, but it had to be. Right?

He recalled how she'd taken off the mask after she'd gotten into the cab. That last smile, light and easy only in appearance. Her eyes had said so much more. She'd pushed him away, taken control to protect herself. He'd walked right into it, because he didn't want to hurt or scare her. But by doing so, he'd sent her the opposite message he'd wanted to send. Who the fuck cared where they would both be in a week? It was what he wanted her to carry around with her for the next year that was important.

"Matt," he said abruptly, slamming down his glass. "I need your help."

There were many reasons to appreciate having lots of money, and the ability to find information quickly was one of them. By waking one of Matt's contacts, they'd found out she was flying back to Fort Bragg in the morning. From there she would return to Iraq. She was with the 18th Theatre Support Command, a Supply Sergeant.

Peter's heart had flipped at that news. While he treated women soldiers with respect, at heart level, he preferred women not to serve in combat areas. It went against his deepest instincts to put a woman in harm's way. Protecting them was a man's job.

Ruefully, he imagined what colorful things Dana would say to that. He was sure she had a mouth on her. Anyone who'd been out in that godforsaken heat, with sand in every crevice and crack, was comfortably fluent in swearing. And of course thinking about her mouth got him hard again, remembering what he'd done with those moist, accommodating lips.

So here he was, standing in the local airport at the security check-in point. He'd gotten there four hours ahead of schedule to be sure, and been scoping it ever since. As intently as he was scanning every face, he was surprised airport security hadn't questioned him.

Though he hadn't seen her without the mask, he knew her the second he saw her. She had only one carry-on, one of those bags women wore slung across their chests to carry all their girl stuff.

Probably a paperback book or some other way to pass the time on the flight. He wondered what she read, what she liked. She was in the jeans he'd seen last night, but now she wore a long-sleeved, snug knit shirt over it with a vee neck that showed the right amount of cleavage. Whatever bra she was wearing was holding her high and firm. A small silver cross nestled between her collarbones.

The face he hadn't demanded to see last night was delicate and determined. She carried her head with graceful dignity on the slim neck, her closely shorn hair only emphasizing the beauty of her skull shape, the sharp slope of cheekbones. A straight nose and lush, soft lips. The conditioning of her body made her movements graceful, confident. Men and women alike couldn't help a second look, because confidence turned a handsome, petite woman into a beautiful, elegant one. With amusement, he saw she was wearing sizable wedges. He wondered if she put platforms in her combat boots to give her the extra five inches she'd tried to use as one of her many defenses last night.

Maybe he was lucky that he'd had so much experience with women, though if she was feeling an ounce of the possessiveness he was, Dana might not think so. All the submissives whose company he'd enjoyed, even the longer relationships he'd had, had taught him not to confuse hormones with his heart. But he saw her and, God, it was exactly like last night. Everything he'd learn about this particular woman would fascinate him; he was sure of it. He'd want to learn more and more. This was real. But that lack of doubt couldn't erase the panicked pressure in his chest, knowing he needed more time. He'd take anything, even thirty minutes in a coffee shop, but she was running late. So he'd have to treat the next ten minutes as the most important of his life—without scaring the shit out of her.

She saw him. As she slowed, cocking her head, her eyes bright with a mixture of curiosity and not a little apprehension, he straightened off the column where he'd been leaning.

"Come here," he mouthed, need burning through him like an oil fire.

How had he found her? Had she conjured him? For the past twelve hours, she'd tried to shake it off. Finally, she'd given up, basking in the freaking glow of the most amazing experience she'd ever had. Why hadn't she given him her address, asked for his?

Because it was best to leave it at one magical night, not spoil it. The fact that it was the most earth-shattering experience she'd ever had sexually, on a deep, emotional level, didn't mean that could translate outside of the club walls. The things that were different about the two of them were still different. Last night had overflowed with magical trappings, perfect timing, everything. That wasn't real. In a real world, Cinderella had to go back to being Cinderella the next day.

She was depressingly aware that such internal arguments said more about her than the experience. Maybe the reason she hadn't found the Dom she'd been seeking was she wasn't brave enough for that risk. She couldn't bear to lose someone she loved again, whether it was from a relationship disintegrating or something far worse. So one night and one night only. That was the best thing.

She'd almost convinced herself of it; then she saw him there. That look, the way he called her to him, those firm lips mouthing the command, and her mind went AWOL.

She didn't know if she walked or ran. She just knew within three seconds she was pressed up against him, on her toes to reach that mouth. *This is crazy, this is crazy, this is crazy. But God, so wonderful.* He cinched his arm around her waist and hauled her up so she could lock her arms around his neck, drink deep, pull him inside her one more time. Leaning back against the column to give them both an anchor, he cupped her head, taking control of the kiss.

All that tall, hard body, so broad and strong, and now she could grip his biceps, run her fingernails over the *Don't Tread On Me* tattoo, scrape his skin. He growled in her mouth but she couldn't resist trailing her fingers through the short hair at his nape as well, letting her hand slide down along his jaw. He made that kiss last a good long time, so long that it was she who had to break it, reluctantly. When he at last let her down to her feet, he kept his hands at her waist, thrilling her with the possessive grip.

"I'm already late for check-in," she said, cursing the fact she was late. "I can't miss this one. I'm due back at the base."

"I know." His mouth became a determined line. "Dana, I expect to see you again."

From the flicker in his gaze, she wondered if he'd intended to use more charm, though the raw honesty hit her low and hard. She knew so little of him. Maybe his cock was just tied up with his head. Maybe her mind was no better, spinning with hormones. She couldn't make this leap right now. She couldn't. She wasn't ready.

But the feelings swelling up now at the look in his gray eyes, his hands on her body, had her rattled down to her toes. She'd been blown away last night. Didn't matter if it was hormones or not—she couldn't deny that she'd never reacted to a man like this, not in her whole life. She'd fantasized about a Master like him, right? So how much could she risk of herself to see if he was the real deal? How far would he go to prove it?

"Okay," she said softly. "Then write to me. Not e-mail. Letters." Old-fashioned love letters, like the ones Gram had gotten from

Grandpa when he was in Vietnam. She'd requested those letters be buried with her.

He studied her, his expression intent, fathomless. "You going to give me an address?"

"You knew to find me here. I expect you can find that easily enough."

"You're not going to write me back, are you?" At her quick negative shake, his gaze darkened, that chin getting an obstinate look she knew she'd be powerless to resist.

"I'll look forward to every one you send me. If it's meant to be, I'll see you again. Please," she added desperately as he slid his touch up her waist, his thumbs pressing into her rib cage beneath her breasts. "It's too much, too soon. I...can't handle it any other way." *Please, please write to me.*

Leaning down, he brushed her nose with his lips, gave her a close-up of those intense eyes once more. "A test. You want me to prove something to you, protect yourself, okay. I'll let you have your way this once, because I don't want you rattled where you're going. But in a year or so, when they let you come home again, you'd better be ready for me, little girl. We're not done. Not by a long shot. And you won't be calling the shots then."

Dana ran her knuckles down his jaw, loving his words, loving that he thought of her safety at the same time he wouldn't let her think she'd gotten away with anything. "Thanks, Captain," she whispered.

So many things she wanted came bubbling up, closing her throat. Maybe if she had enough faith, she would give him everything about her, inside and out. Despite the family she no longer had, she wanted to believe the crazy idea that this virtual stranger could be her new family. She wanted someone in the world to know her down to the deepest level of her soul, be connected to her in a way that even death couldn't take. She wanted him to be that someone.

God. Which was exactly why it was best to do it this way. If he was the real deal, blurting all that out right now would surely send him into full retreat, back out to the overpriced parking. Right? When he put his hand to her face, that thought vanished. Turning her cheek toward that tender gesture, she leaned into his hand, letting him hold her that way, hoping she was conveying...something to him. Something that would make it worth it to him to keep writing, even when she wouldn't let herself write back, the most unfair test possible.

"I hate this." His jaw flexed. "I want to keep you safe."

Giving him a smile, she picked up his other hand, opened it. She bent his middle and index fingers inward, leaving the other fingers straight. Tapping those two fingers on her chest, she curled her hand over his. Her fist barely covered his, but she squeezed him hard nevertheless.

"That's sign language for heart. You'll hold my heart safe until I see you again." She swallowed, whispered the next word. "Master." His eyes became molten at the title, spoken outside the restrictions of the club, making her glad she'd dared that much. Rising on her toes, she pressed her cheek to his strong jaw, closed her eyes and let herself be totally vulnerable this blink in time, holding their locked hands between them. "Keep your ass down, too. I haven't seen nearly as much of it as I want to. But...if you change your mind about us, thanks for everything."

"I'm not changing my mind."

"I hope so. But no obligations, Captain Peter Winston."

It was so hard to move out of that embrace. Somehow it tied into everyone and everything to whom she'd ever had to say good-bye. She was blinking back freaking tears. Shouldering her bag, she gave him a quick nod and moved toward check-in.

Instead of making forward progress, however, she was brought up short, the strap of her bag used to haul her back up against him one more time. He invaded her with a kiss that reached all the way to her toes, caused her to cling and sigh into his mouth, perilously close to saying words that would make her a romantic fool.

When he let her up for air, he held her gaze like an oath.

"You got an obligation to me, Sergeant. And I won't be forgetting it."

CHAPTER FOUR

Two months later

"*M*an, I can't believe I'm in this fucking oven on wheels with you two when Gary Sinise is coming to visit our platoon today. I wanted to squeeze Lieutenant Dan's fine, tight ass." Specialist Leslie Sykes peered out over the rocky desert terrain. "I see you snickering back there, O'Neill. I know you're still chasing that tail up at Battalion, so don't think you're better than me."

"Nope. No more. I realized a man has to be an idiot to get involved with a heavily armed woman."

"Good thinking. No woman in her right mind could hang out with you for more than ten minutes and not want to shoot you," Dana said, keeping her eye on their right perimeter, tracking the vehicles behind them. "Of course, you'd best remember women are resourceful. If they don't have a gun, a blunt object works mighty fine. More personal that way."

Leslie laughed. "Sounds like you might be better off switch ing sides of the fence, O'Neill. Come squeeze Lieutenant Dan's ass with me."

"Hey, hey, hey..." O'Neill gave her a mock scowl. "Don't ask, don't tell, soldier." He jerked his chin at Dana. "She's just running a diversion. She doesn't want us poking at her about that guy she's been mooning over ever since she got back."

Dana shifted in the passenger seat, adjusting her helmet. "I only want you poking at me, Sergeant O'Neill. You and all your fine manly stuff."

Leslie snorted. "Like I believe that. I think he's got your number, girlfriend. What's this boy like?"

Dana smirked. "A tall, blond captain with an ass that would put anything you've ever imagined to shame. The ass of all asses."

"Ooh, she's gone to the white-boy side." Leslie chuckled. "Your grandma would be spinning."

"No. I think she would have liked him."

Her own certainty about that surprised her. He'd written her, as he'd promised. Once a week, without fail. While those letters should have come with a fire-hazard warning, they were devastating for far more than the sexual innuendoes...

I can't believe I agreed to this shit. One minute I feel like some lovesick fool; then I remember that kiss, the way you ran to me at the airport, and I can barely breathe. Yeah, it's crazy. I know you're trying to convince yourself it's hormones, that I'm writing this because I'm seeing way too many sweaty guys and not enough soft, female flesh, but it's you, Dana. I don't want to be a dick, but that night was far from the first time for me. But it was the first time I was left with this hurting ache inside. Letting you go was a mistake, leaving an emptiness that won't be filled until I see you again. Are we both crazy? I want to find out. I intend to find out.

I know you were scared, and that's part of why you decided to make us do it this way. I don't want you to be scared, sweetheart. I want to know everything about you, why you're so scared of loving and losing. But I'm thinking you're also pretty smart, because I'm writing all sorts of things I wouldn't normally share with a woman, especially if I want her to remain impressed with me. For example, I like little dogs. Particularly the scrapper ones, the Jack Russells, who won't give up and are so tough they won't back down from anything. Kittens are pretty irresistible, too. My buddy Lucas and his wife, Cass, just got a couple from the shelter and they're maniacs, tearing up everything while making them laugh their asses off.

I guess I'm pretty predictable. Beer and pizza is my favorite meal, and I like falling asleep in my boat on the bayou. I once woke up beached on a sand spit next to a couple alligators. They apparently figured I was too dumb to mess with. I'd like to fall asleep in my boat with you in my arms, let the sun bake us and not wake up until the mosquitoes try to drive us in...no alligators that trip, though.

If I told you I started falling in love with you the first moment I saw you, the kind of fall that could turn into a lifetime of love worth having, it would scare you to death, wouldn't it? So I won't say it. I'll just think it.

Her lips curved in a small smile, remembering. They'd had nothing more than sex between them, right? But as if that was a battle already fought and won, his letters cut right past the bullshit, letting her into his mind, telling her his thoughts. He was drawing her in, making her want to be with him on all levels so bad that it hurt, just like he said.

I've always wanted to drive across the country, stop wherever we wanted. See those sights that nobody ever takes the time to see. The best ice cream shop in a small town in the middle of Iowa, run by two people who started it back during the fifties. Or a historical marker where some famous Civil War general watered his horse and sat under a tree, writing a letter to his wife. I think you find out a lot about someone when you travel with them. And though our initial trip was way too short, I already know I'd like to take a much, much longer one together. Don't shake your head. I know that's what you're doing. So how about it? I'm going to finish every letter with a question, because I want you to have all sorts of answers for me when next we see each other...but one will be more important than any of the others.

"I've got movement to the left," O'Neill said sharply.

Dana's attention snapped fully back to the present, though even with the distraction of Peter's letters, the forefront of her mind had never left off surveillance of their surroundings. Vehicles moving supplies between towns were too rich of a target, and Combat Logistic Patrols ran every day to supply Combat Outpost Posts. The up-armored FMTV lumbering behind them carried medical and food supplies. In front of their vehicle was Sergeant Sinclair's up-armored Humvee, and two more followed behind the FMTV.

"Where?" Leslie asked, and then the question became moot. Dana shouted out the warning as the RPG round whistled through the air. The rear vehicle of their convoy exploded, the flash illuminating the area.

In a matter of seconds, everything was chaos. They'd hit a straight stretch between two curves, and the insurgents had set their ambush well. The sergeant and his detail ahead barely made it out before their vehicle exploded, blockading forward progress. A hail of AK-47 gunfire rained down from the ridge on their three o'clock. It was a sure bet they'd mined the sides of the road with IEDs to keep them from going around.

Fortunately, they hadn't gotten the Humvee that mounted a 50-cal, right behind the FMTV. Those guys were firing hot and heavy up into that ridge.

"Go, go, go," O'Neill was barking. Dana slid out after Leslie and they hit the hard-packed ground, running for the meager ditch on the opposite side of the road.

"Straighten up." Dana grabbed Leslie's vest and hauled her along. Leslie rarely got out of the Battalion S4 shop and had made a newbie mistake, trying to crouch down as she ran. The body armor was too heavy to allow for that. She'd trip and land on her face. "Move your ass!"

The dirt kicked up around them as they ran, but Dana heard the M-4 fire as O'Neill covered their six. In the corner of her eye, she saw the men in the Humvee and supply truck doing the same, a gradual fall back to this ditch line.

"Targets ahead." Dana heard the shout, saw the insurgents waiting in the ditch, guns raised, dark eyes wild, faces wet with nervous sweat. She swung her own gun around, braced for recoil and let it go, sending them scattering. One got punched through the head and flipped back, and then she and Leslie were in the ditch and she was shoving the body out of the way.

"Breathe, girl, breathe," she counseled Leslie, hunkering down. "Just keep it together, shoot straight and wait for orders. They'll call for air support."

And please God, let them get here in time.

"God, no women in combat. Yeah, right." Though Leslie's voice was cracking, Dana was glad to see she was keeping it together, checking her ammo with shaking fingers. Then her gaze landed on something else sharing the ditch with them.

"Les, look."

Her friend followed her gaze, saw the RPG left behind by the fleeing insurgents on this side. "I've never shot one."

"Me neither." Dana firmed her chin. "We'll sure as hell figure it out. That Humvee only has a few minutes before someone throws a mortar on it."

"Us, too, probably. Fuck. God, this is crazy."

Thankfully it wasn't Dana's first firefight, so the rapid change of circumstances and incredible noise wasn't new to her. There was no communication down the line yet, the sergeant likely trying to raise that air support and relying on their knowledge of how to stay down until he decided how to form their defensive line. Right now, this was likely the best they could do.

Snatching up the weapon, Dana examined it closely, figured out the dual trigger. She had to wiggle up the side of the ditch. Bullets cut through the ground at the edge. But setting her teeth, she went to her knees, lifted her helmeted head and took aim.

The missile shot up. She'd aimed lower than her target. As she'd anticipated, it went higher than she'd intended, but not too high. It hit the ridge a couple feet below the edge. Dirt and rock exploded, sending an avalanche of debris and flailing bodies down.

"O'Neill," Leslie screamed.

Dana tossed the RPG aside. O'Neill had gotten briefly pinned down at the vehicles, providing additional cover fire for the drivers. When he made a run for it, a round hit him from the insurgents who'd come out from the hidden curve ahead. He dropped like a stone.

The two women didn't hesitate, coming up over the edge of the ditch shoulder to shoulder. "Get him to cover," Dana shouted, turning the M-4 toward that group of targets along with the others who came to back her up. Leslie grabbed hold of him, tried to get him onto his feet, but O'Neill was six feet of muscle. Another soldier went to help. Dana backpedaled in front of them, bullets whistling around her, kicking up dirt. Thank God, the insurgents were probably jacked up on adrenaline shots or Khat, not shooting worth shit, but it was close enough. Any second she expected one to punch through her. Noise and AK-47 fire, hell on earth.

She had been in active engagement before because of situations like this, but nothing this intense. She'd trained for it, though, and kept training for it, even more so than the guys who got field experience far more often. The enemy didn't give a damn if you were a woman or not when it came to shooting U.S. soldiers, and this situation made all those extra grueling hours of practice worth it, even if her heart was pounding up in her ears.

Think about the targets, and a gorgeous captain who will be so *pissed if you don't come home and take that cross-country trip with him. Nap in that boat together. He'd probably chase you to the Pearly Gates with those alligators just to beat your ass.*

She stumbled over something, saw a Pepsi bottle roll away wildly. A second later, the world exploded in bright light and pain.

CHAPTER FIVE

One year later

*P*eter got out of the taxi and breathed deep of the bayou that backed up to his Baton Rouge home. Jon had been coming here regularly while Peter was on tour so it didn't get an empty feeling to it. While that meant he'd probably burned some weird incense or had one of his tranquil and oh-so-centered bedmates chant over the front door, that was okay. Whatever he did, Peter had no doubt it would feel as comfortable as when he left. This time it was going to feel better than it ever had. Not only because it was home, but because now he could go after Dana.

Fourteen months had gone by, and his feelings ran as strong for her as they had that night. Worse, even. It was the damnedest thing, but why should he be surprised? Matt and Lucas had known the minute they met Savannah and Cass, respectively. He'd seen it happen, but hadn't realized it felt like this.

He couldn't believe he'd agreed to her terms, satisfying himself with a one-way stream of letters until the end of their tour. As he'd told her, sometimes he'd felt like a lovesick fool, putting his thoughts in that vacuum. But he kept himself going by reviewing, again and again, every detail of their short time together. Particularly how she'd seen him in the airport and run to him like water in the desert. She'd surrendered to him that night at The Zone, and not merely her flesh. When she kissed him, there'd been forever in that girl's grip.

The second he got stateside, he'd called Jon, asking him to find out where she was and have Matt's admin make travel arrangements for him. He didn't care if she considered that cheating. *His* tour was done. He was going to have a shower and a nap, but twenty-four hours weren't going to pass before he was on his way to her. Thank God for the Taliban and dangerous missions. They'd kept him from going crazy this past year.

Smiling wryly, he opened the front door, and found Jon sitting in his living room. With Matt, Lucas and Ben, suggesting they'd all ridden together in Jon's car out front.

Peter stopped. They would have met up tonight for beers and celebrated his return, but they wouldn't have come like this. Not unless...

When Jon rose, the expression in his somber face twisted Peter's gut. "She's dead." Peter forced out the words, but a heartbeat later cursed himself for being the one to say what he least wanted to hear. "That's not possible. The letters didn't come back."

"They were forwarded. She's not dead, Peter." Jon took a step forward. Peter held his ground, his fists clenching. Waiting. "She was injured in southern Iraq twelve months ago. She's been stateside ever since."

"Is she... What happened to her? Is her family..."

He should have done everything to keep her off that plane, sacrificed a lifetime of principles and patriotism to keep her safe. He was going to shake Jon like a rag doll if he didn't start talking. *Now.*

"It was a firefight, a pretty bad one," Jon said, holding him with his steady gaze as Lucas moved to Peter's side. "She got caught in an explosion when she was laying down cover fire."

Damn it, Sergeant. You're not supposed to be in combat. But women never did as they were told, did they? He'd seen the jut of the stubborn chin, the firm muscle of that lean, prepared body. She wouldn't walk away from a fight. No more than he would.

"What's happened to her?"

"She's blind." Peter closed his eyes, but Jon pressed on, knowing him well enough to give him all of it, fast as possible. "She lost the ability to hear in one ear. The other has diminished capacity. She's badly scarred, but my understanding is most can be repaired with reconstructive surgery. Some of it has already been done. But the main thing is she's alive, she can walk and she has all fingers, toes and limbs. Focus on that."

43

"Okay." Peter nodded, his lips folded together tight. While he told his heart to stop thundering, the other men drew closer, forming a half ring around him. That, plus the hesitation in Jon's voice, tipped him off to the fact he hadn't heard it all.

"Tell me the rest." Peter shifted his gaze to Matt, standing directly in front of him. Years ago, Matt had been the one to come and tell the younger man his parents had been killed in a car crash. The steady look in his gaze had been the same then, despite the fact Matt had barely been out of college himself. Kensington would do whatever it took to get a job done. To make things right. He'd honed the same quality in Peter.

"Dana has no living family," Matt said quietly. "She had no support system to deal with this."

"You tell me she's on the street talking to herself, living out of the garbage, and I'm going to have to kill somebody."

"No." Lucas put a hand on his shoulder. "She didn't have much in the way of a bank account, but she got full disability and benefits, enough to rent a small place near a VA hospital and cover her living expenses. She's not going to be vacationing in Tahiti every year, but she's not starving. She's high up on the list for care at a residential facility, but they're crowded, and in truth, the specialist I talked to said she doesn't need that."

Peter's pulse thudded anew against his throat. "So why's she on the list?"

Jon shook his head. "She's doing the minimum required to learn new skills, improve the compensatory use of her other senses. The specialist confided that it was the nurses who coordinated the duplex unit where she's living. They found a lady, a nurse, to stay next door and take care of her. I'm sorry, Peter, but I know you'd want to know. He said if not for those steps, she might very well have ended up on the street. She has no interest in anything other than sitting in a chair."

"Damn it, they have all sorts of resources for PTSD shit. Why didn't they—?"

"The patient has to be willing. And you know how irreplaceable a family support network is for dealing with those kinds of issues." Jon swept a meaningful glance among the men standing before him. "Which is why we're here now."

Peter swallowed, pushing down the fury, the knowledge that still had his pulse accelerated. Lucas squeezed his shoulder, a reminder of support. Taking a deep breath, he thought it through, closing his eyes again to focus.

They waited him out. He was the hands-on guy, the one who went and straightened out snarls at plants in their Central and South American locations, dealing with a wide variety of concerns in unexpected, sometimes volatile, environments. If he approached it that way, he wouldn't lose his head, get mired down in thoughts about how she needed him and he wasn't at her side right now.

He opened his eyes. "I need to know everything you know, Jon. I want to talk to this specialist myself. I'm bringing her home."

Ben raised a brow. "You knew her for one night."

"It doesn't matter," Matt answered for Peter, gazing into his face. "She's the one, isn't she?"

Peter nodded. All those months, he hadn't doubted his emotions, though their strength had baffled him. Now, on a tidal surge of those feelings, thinking about where she was, how she needed him, he knew what it was. The men around him, they were the family he'd chosen, but she was like a part of his heart that had been missing since he'd lost his blood family. A part sent by fate, so he'd recognized her from that first second.

He shook his head, holding that back before it unmanned him. "Since she's coming back here with me, whether she likes the idea or not, it's likely I'll need some wheels greased."

"Always happy to keep you out of jail for kidnapping," Ben said dryly.

Matt moved forward then. Lucas withdrew so Matt's hand could replace his, grip Peter's shoulder with hard reassurance. "We'll take care of both of you. Bring her home."

CHAPTER SIX

*A*s individuals, they were relentless. As a team, they couldn't be stopped. It had taken a few nerve-racking days to get it all together, but if they could pull off an aggressive takeover of a floundering multinational corporation, they could handle the relocation of one female soldier, willing or not. Paperwork wasn't a problem for Ben. But then they hit an unexpected snag. A determined, caring woman.

Christina Lawson was a retired RN, a former Vietnam field nurse. Her husband had killed himself years ago, never able to leave Vietnam behind. She was the one who lived in the other side of the duplex and checked on Dana daily. She rebuffed Ben's legal bullshit, charming persuasions and veiled threats alike.

So Jon stepped in, because Peter's impatience made diplomacy impossible. While he didn't know what Jon had said to her, she at last agreed to their plan to relocate her charge. *If* she had a face-to-face meeting with Peter first, and *if* Dana consented to leave with him.

Peter wasn't going to fault the woman for being protective of Dana. But when he stepped out of the rental car in front of the small duplex, a nondescript housing unit located adjacent to the hospital acreage, he was vibrating with the need to kick in the door of whichever side held Dana, and say to hell with any more delays. Since Christina Lawson was planted on the porch, arms akimbo, his plan might have to include a wrestling match with a woman old enough to be a grandmother.

As he came up the walk, the nurse studied him from head to toe, her expression suggesting she was considering whether she needed a broom or a shotgun. He cleared his throat, made a considerable effort to look affable and charming, despite the ache that had been building inside him these interminable five days. It was now threatening to hemorrhage.

"Mr. Winston?" Christina offered a hand and he closed his over it, noting fingers swollen with early arthritis, but there was strength there still. She nodded toward the porch swing. "We can talk here."

No "glad to meet you," or other bland courtesies that would mean nothing to either one of them. He could appreciate that, but the knot in his stomach didn't loosen.

"Won't she...?"

Christina shook her head. "I told her I was going to be on the porch, visiting with a friend of mine. She rarely gets out of her day chair, so I knew we'd have enough time for privacy. She wears her hearing aid grudgingly, so she won't hear us, either. Even if she has it on, she has to concentrate on what's being said and the person must speak clearly, toward the functioning ear, for her to detect and understand. Unfortunately, visual clues and lip reading are what help a person with hearing loss the most, and those are aids her blindness denies her."

"I'll get her upgraded to a top-of-the-line hearing aid," he said immediately. Jon had already told him about advances in technology, which he'd heard with only half an ear, but Peter remembered the basics nonetheless.

Christina cocked her head. "The problem isn't money, Mr. Winston. Money undoubtedly helps, but there are impoverished children blind and deaf as Helen Keller who adapt to their handicaps. The problem is her. I think you already know that, though. Please sit."

He took a seat, bracing the swing when his weight tipped it forward. A tight smile touched Christina's features, but he wasn't sure if he could be encouraged by it.

"You are a big man, that's for certain. Mr. Forte said you were a businessman, but you have military written all over you."

"I just finished my Afghanistan tour."

"I know that. I know a lot more about you than you realize, Mr. Winston." She was on her hip on the swing, her sneakered feet swaying lightly over the boards as he unconsciously moved the swing in an agitated rhythm. Noticing it, he stopped, but she continued to study him, saying nothing.

Goddamn it, he was going to go insane. "Tell me what you need to know, Mrs. Lawson." Turning to face her dead on, he dropped any pretense at hiding how he felt. "How do I get past you? I've waited fourteen months to be back with her again. She may not have said a single word about me, but I can tell you, right before I shipped out, she opened her heart to me, and I'm sure she's as much mine as I'm hers. I won't do anything to hurt her. I swear it to you on everything I am. You want blood, a written guarantee—"

He stopped, his jaw flexing. "I'm sorry. I know I sound like an obsessive stalker. I'm just... I'm going fu— I'm going insane not being close to her, able to help her. You've done a great job; I'm grateful, but—"

"That's fine, Mr. Winston," Christina said abruptly. "I've seen what I need to know. Here are my terms. You can stay the night here with Dana. In the morning, if she tells me she wants to go with you, she can of course go wherever she wishes."

Now it was his turn to stare at her. "That's it?"

The nurse nodded. He blinked, ran a hand over his face. "Well, I'm sorry, Mrs. Lawson. The way you were over the phone with Jon... Hell, the way you looked when I pulled up, I was expecting a hell of a lot more than that."

"You expected me to pull out the interrogation techniques I learned in Saigon?" She twinkled at him then, but the humor didn't reach her eyes.

"Yeah, a little. Do you mind if I ask what miracle changed your mind?"

"It was not so much what you did to change my mind, as what you did to confirm the decision I'd already made. Can I trust you to stay here?"

Under that penetrating maternal stare, he was hard-pressed not to squirm, but he nodded. Pursing her lips together, she rose and disappeared into the right-hand side, taking care not to let the screen door slam. When she returned, she held a decorative photo box. As she opened the top, Peter saw his letters, neatly filed. At his stunned look, Christina nodded.

"I can't get her to do much. Not even basic navigation of her surroundings, but she always knows where this box is. She shows no interest in anything, but she'll do almost anything I ask, if I agree to read one to her. Though I don't know why that matters, because her lips move as I read them. She knows them all by heart."

Peter's gaze strayed back to the box. There were worn places in the glossy veneer, where it looked as though fingers had gripped it, often. Christina watched him. "Some nights, when I'm wandering about out here, smoking a cigarette—a terrible habit I've never kicked —I'll see her sitting in her bedroom, dark but for the television. She'll be holding that box, or have one of your letters in her hand, stroking her fingers over the words she can't see."

Because Peter remembered some of the things he'd put in those letters, it was an effort to hold that knowing gaze, but she was continuing. "I've cared for many soldiers since my husband. I have no degree in psychology. Sometimes I think all that learning can interfere with seeing with your heart, using your common sense. But I do know when they lose interest in everything, turn so deep inside themselves that not even the ones who love them most can reach them, they're already in the grave." Her voice wavered, old shadows rising in her eyes, but she firmed her chin.

"Dana is like that in so many ways, except for this. You are her one lifeline, Peter. For the chance that it can save her, I will risk throwing that line to you, a man I only know through these letters, but who has come to me and spoken from his heart."

Her green light made him want to leap up, shove through that door, but she was his best key to reaching Dana's mind. "Why do you think she's drawn into herself?"

She shook her head. "It's hard enough when you have family to support you. But when you go through this and wake up so alone and isolated... Her grandmother was her last living family, and she died three years ago. Dana had two brothers, both killed in gang wars on the streets, though apparently she was the eldest and tried to keep them out of trouble. Her mother ran off on them and she didn't know her father. A common enough tale for a girl born in bad circumstances. Thanks to her grandmother, she made something of herself."

The nurse glanced over the quiet neighborhood street again. "Our girl in there protected a fallen comrade under heavy fire. She didn't have to do it, but she did it anyway. She was given a medal at Walter Reed. The nurses packed it with her belongings, but she hasn't touched it." She sighed. "I'd lay money she's never been a whiner or shirker in her whole life. But a woman who's had to be so self-reliant can break when she's pushed hard enough. When she thinks she's all alone."

"She had you."

"There's a difference between that, and having someone who's close to her heart, someone who *knows* her heart, to help her heal. That is what I got from your letters, Captain Winston. I think you know her heart, by instinct if not experience. I honestly feel that all that Dana needs is someone with a key to her. I don't think she's in a deep depression, the kind that they treat with chemicals. She's angry a lot, and anger means passion. Apathy and indifference are much worse signs."

She took a breath. "If you can get to her, and she puts half the energy to getting out of her chair that she dedicates to staying in it, she'll do as much as she ever planned to do, and probably more. All she needs is someone to help her find herself again. Once she does that, the rest—learning new skills, rehabilitation—it's all waiting for her. I expect you'll help her through that, but if you need guidance, I'm always willing to point you in the right direction."

She rose as abruptly as she'd done everything else, a woman of decisive action. Peter expected she'd been a hell of a field nurse. "All right, then. She's all yours. Unless you come and get me next door, you won't be disturbed until tomorrow morning."

"But—" Sudden panic invaded him.

Christina reached out and took his hand, an unexpected reassurance, her brisk voice gentling. "There's nothing medically wrong with her, Peter. Except for the fact she barely eats or moves out of that chair, she's as healthy as you are. And she knows enough about her handicaps to let you know before you take a misstep. You'll be fine."

She withdrew her touch and straightened. "Be what you know she needs you to be. Kick her ass into gear again. She doesn't need any pity. She's had way too much of that. I'm going to go grocery shopping now, but I'll be back in a while. Trial by fire. I understand that's your specialty."

Giving him one more direct look, she put the box quietly inside Dana's door, retrieved purse and keys from her own unit, and headed down the walkway to her car.

∾

She doesn't need any pity. Jesus. He understood that, but all he wanted to do was scoop Dana up, rock her in his lap and tell her he was going to take care of everything. He was still wrestling with it when he stepped into her unit, made his way through a bland front room and functional kitchen, to the back den where Christina had indicated she spent most of her daylight hours.

When he stepped into the room, conflicting emotions swamped him.

Except for what was filtering through the sheer panels, there was no light. It made it a soft, sad atmosphere, adding to what vibrated from the woman curled up on an oversized recliner. Since she appeared to be staring toward the window, he suspected she had some sense of the light, or perhaps she felt the sun's heat. Though it was afternoon, she wore pajama bottoms and a sweatshirt that swallowed her. She looked clean and showered, however. Since she still kept her hair short, the filtered light gleamed off the slender tube that wound around the shell of her ear to hold the hearing aid in place.

She'd turned into a mole. Burrowing down in her clothes, her recliner, her featureless home, digging a hole to bury herself here. *Jesus Christ.* Christina was right. He didn't need a shrink's license to understand the less-than-subtle message.

I wish I'd died, rather than having to face this alone.

In that revelation, pity got shoved to the side by something much stronger in him. Anger. It didn't matter that it wasn't at her, or that it might be misplaced. He'd use it.

There was plenty of room for him on the recliner, so he settled his hip there, his thigh close to the tips of her bare brown toes. They were painted deep burgundy. That had to be Christina's doing. Laying his palm over them, he closed his hand instinctively over the small, cold digits, passing his thumb over her sole.

Her head lifted and turned toward him, the light from the window showing him more of her face. The sightless eyes wrenched his gut, made him want to weep. As Jon had said, they'd done their best to repair the extensive scarring in her face, but it would take time for the surgical scars to heal and disappear. She would never again have the fresh, sculpted beauty she'd had that night. It had been replaced by a hard, tortured thinness. But as much as that and the lack of vision in her eyes concerned him, it was the lack of fire that bothered him most. Her gaze wasn't merely sightless, but also lifeless.

No. Christina had said she had passion, anger. That fire was only dormant. He would accept nothing less. *Know her heart by instinct.* He was no Prince Charming, but he'd spent a great deal of his sexually mature years learning to uncover a woman's inner sensuality and fan it to a raging inferno. For a submissive, that reaction was so closely linked to her soul, both had to be ignited to give her everything she needed. So maybe he did have the key. Because from their one night together, he knew what kind of submissive she was.

Reaching out, he put his palm on the side of her face. As she had at the airport, she tilted her head into it, her eyes closing. No matter the scars, her sweet mouth, the curve of her cheek, her slim neck, they were all the same. Tracing her lips with his thumb, he teased them open to caress her teeth, graze her tongue. She tasted him with the tip of it, and he saw a lethargic desire flicker across her face.

"I keep dreaming about you." Her voice was a bit raspy. There'd been some damage to her vocal cords, but if he hadn't known, it would have passed as a sexy purr. The volume was a little low, the pronunciation slurred, as if she were sleepy. "That night. I want to be back there with you, so much. God. It was all so physical, and so much more than that. I ache when I think about you, Master." She swallowed and became a smaller ball, as if compressing her thighs and the need there. "I'd rather dream about being with you forever, than live another single day, you know?"

She used his hand as a pillow, nestling down farther. With her other hand she splayed his fingers, ran them over her mouth, one at a time, slow, tasting, nuzzling. Peter felt his groin tighten, even as he was appalled at himself. She's...

There's nothing medically wrong with her, Peter. Christina's admonition, her knowing look. Wow, he was slow on the uptake. But he was still warring with it, the need to nurture and yet take her over at once. Hold her close and spank her within an inch of her life for scaring him. Well, hell, there was time for both, wasn't there?

Her brow was crinkling, mouth pressing together as if holding back emotion. "God, it smells like you, feels like you. The heat in your skin. Gram used to tell me I could have anything I wanted bad enough, do whatever I wanted to do." A bitter chuckle. "That's what we tell kids, don't we? It gives them the courage to try. But what do we say when they end up like this? No 'Be All You Can Be' Army slogan now, hmm?"

Peter pressed his lips together. Taking his hand away, he bracketed her with an arm, leaned in until the heat of his breath touched her face and she lifted hers, startled at his proximity.

"It's time to cut this shit out, Sergeant."

She jerked up. He was quick enough she didn't slam into his chin, but he didn't go far. Paling, she touched the front of his shirt, then moved to his arms, feeling the cant of his body over hers. "Peter? Oh, fucking hell, I thought..."

"Been talking to me a lot without me being here? Living in your own reality?" He caught one of her seeking hands, squeezed it a little harder than he wanted to.

"You can't be here." She snatched her hand back, retreated as much as the cushioning would allow, as if she was trying to burrow there in truth. "You don't want this."

He kept her caged between his arms, made her feel the energy of his immovable presence. When he brushed his lips against her cheek, he registered the satisfying ripple of reaction, the pant of her nervous breath. "Telling me what I want isn't your job, Sergeant. That's the problem you had the night we met. You tried to control the uncontrollable."

Her lip curled, but he smelled fear behind the sudden anger. "What's my job, Captain? School crossing guard? Airline pilot?"

"That's self-pitying crap. There's more than that out there. But for right now, you only have one job. Doing whatever I tell you to do. You're going home with me."

Shock flitted across her face, followed by desperation, warring between fury and frustration. Hope dodged in between, so ghostlike it broke his heart. But he also saw something else, a lick of lust, his order igniting something deeper and more primal in her, something that had made her surrender to him over a year ago. But now her fingers curled into tight balls, fighting him.

"Not much difference between my self-pity and your pity. You're not taking me home like some kind of stray that needs your help. You don't want an invalid."

"No." He answered with a calm he didn't feel. "But that's not what you are. There's a difference between an invalid and a person who thinks she's one."

She shoved at him. He let her get out of the chair, but he noted she didn't go far, swaying uncertainly. Damn if Christina wasn't right. Dana had lived here for months, and yet she was barely familiar with her surroundings. When he rose and she lifted her face, he could tell she could gauge his height. Her senses were there. Just waiting for her to fucking use them. She'd said he didn't want her. He noted she hadn't said she didn't want *him* or what he was offering.

"We had a deal, Sergeant, and I'm not letting you out of it," he said sharply. He'd communicated in battle and on a busy manufacturing floor. He had no problem being heard by a woman with hearing aids. "You can't see, or hear as well as you could before. But you can smell, taste...touch. If you've been dreaming about me the way I've been dreaming about you, I know exactly what you've been thinking about. We're going to start there."

He caught her hand. Before she could pull away, he brought it to the front of his jeans, letting her touch wake to life the beast he hadn't sated since he last saw her.

It shocked the hell out of her; he could tell that right off. She hadn't been treated as a woman in a while, a woman from whom a man might demand things like this. A hardcore submissive's desire went beyond sex, into some deeper, psychological matters. He'd use his knowledge of that unapologetically. Maybe knowing less about her personally would help, because it would keep his focus on the one thing that might break her out of this self-imposed funk of hers. Then he could sate his overwhelming desire to give her the tenderness and comfort he had stored to overflowing in him, learn everything he wanted to know about her.

Her face was a study in mixed emotions, but the parted lips, the tension strumming in her body, told him she was reluctantly aroused.

Surprised, he watched her sink down before him, her hands slipping to his upper thighs. Though staying still was excruciating, he waited, seeing what she would do.

Her lips twisted, and now he saw that anger simmering that Christina had warned was there. "I don't have to see to give great head, do I? Even with this face I can be a pretty good whore. Hell, better, because I won't rely on my looks."

Before he gave himself too much time to think it through, Peter pushed her backward onto her ass. She landed hard.

"Ouch," she yelped. When he yanked her up by the front of the shirt, thank God she reacted as he'd hoped. Twisting to break free, she kicked, taking him below the knee. If she'd been in shape, she might have caused him real damage, but in this case it barely registered. Making sure she had her feet under her, he pushed her off him.

She stumbled back and went rigid, stretching her hands out around her, floundering. It killed him, but he forced himself to remain ruthless. "This is what you learned in basic combat training. This weak-assed shit."

Shock coursed her features, but then her face hardened like a weathered statue. "I haven't exactly been keeping combat ready," she snapped.

"Yeah, I noticed. You've been sitting on your ever-widening butt—"

Her temper didn't ignite. It exploded, frustration uncapped in a way he didn't anticipate. Snarling like a wild animal, she swung and overbalanced. He caught her as she fell into him, but immediately tossed her back to her feet rather than gathering her to him the way every cell of him craved to do.

Despite the disorientation, she whirled, baring her teeth. He saw the flash of fire he wanted and kept pushing, ignoring the ache in his own chest. "You can fight. You just won't. You've given up. You're lucky—"

"Not the fucking 'You're lucky' speech again. I swear to God, the next person that says that to me—"

"Will what? Get a tap from that little-girl fist of yours? I'm getting a hard-on from it. Come tickle me some more."

She screamed and lashed out again, but this time she focused.

Her fist landed against his palm, held square in front of his face.

His jaw set in satisfaction. *There's my girl. Would have snapped my head back.* His fingers closed over her tense fingers, holding them as she quivered.

"Damn it. I can't..."

"Yeah." He touched her neck carefully, cupped the side of it, then squeezed, hard. "Yeah, sweetheart, you can. But you need help."

"Not you." She shook her head, and tears seeped out, destroying him. "Not from you. Damn it, Peter, I want to have some pride left."

"You're pissing it away, every day you sit in that chair. You smell like this room, not a human being. You're becoming part of the furniture." He brought her chin up to him, glad she couldn't see the anguish in his face as he made his voice rough. "And you gave up the choice by not accepting help from anyone else. If you *ever* make a crack like that about being a whore again, I will fuck you up ten ways to Sunday. You won't sit comfortably for a month. You're no one's whore."

"I can feel the scars. I look like a monster."

"No, you don't." He moved his palms to her face, to the healing lines at her cheek and forehead, teasing her lashes. "Your eyes are still that pale green, like marsh grass. You've got a surgical scar here, and here...healing. Your skin is still so soft, your lips so full. " He placed one of his hands over her heart, cognizant of the rise and fall of her breast, and one against her temple, stroking the short hair there. "Heart and head. That's all you need to heal, Dana. The rest doesn't matter. It's just skin. You're beautiful to me, inside and out."

"You don't even know me."

"Yeah, I do. That's what scares the shit out of you. I can bust your comfort zone wide-open. I'm not going to leave you alone. I want you to live again."

Her breathing elevated, the tracks of her tears widening. "I want you to leave," she said brokenly.

"No, you don't." He swallowed, hoping it was the truth. "You've always taken care of yourself. You hate depending on others. You think you have to run the whole damn world without help. The only time you let it go is when you follow orders or put on a leash and collar and hand it to the right Master. But even that you had to control, and that's why you never found him, thank God. Until you found me. I'm not going to let you control me. I'm going to help you, no matter how hard you try to drive me away. Starting right now, I'm going to prove that to you."

"How?"

~

Dana didn't have a comfort zone anymore. She had a big, dark hole in which she lived, the definition of isolation. But his presence seemed to shoot light into that hole, and he was right about that part—it scared the shit out of her. She wanted to cringe in the shadows, stay away from those spears of illumination and the pain they could bring. She needed him to be gone. He was supposed to be her fondest memory, not part of her desolate reality.

Instead, he shoved all her wishes aside when he answered her frightened question with action. He caught her under the arms, pushed her against the wall and put his body flush against her, lifting her off her feet.

Oh, God, he felt even better than she remembered. Those same broad shoulders, corded neck. His smell... Oh, she hadn't savored his smell the way she should have. Aftershave, soap, heated, angry male. His testosterone was at boiling point, and having someone angry at her felt incomprehensibly good. She wanted to fight with him some more, draw blood, so much rage boiling to the surface. The passive-aggressive anger she spewed in fits and starts at Christina was nowhere near the clean, white-hot fury that Peter drew to the surface, simmering darkly for so long with no outlet.

He might kiss her. The very thought ignited spiraling pleasure in her lower belly, its potential heat capable of burning the rest away like a big trash burn, the shit that had been roiling in her gut for months. Instead, though, he hiked her up against his body so she had to wrap her stiff, tired legs around his hips. She wasn't sure where he was taking her until he laid her down on her bed. Before she could antici-pate him, he'd stripped her of her pajama bottoms and the cotton panties beneath.

Holy shit. She wasn't ready for this, and she defended herself the only way a helpless animal under attack could. Rolling into a ball, she wrapped her hands in the base of the sweatshirt so he couldn't take it off. She shook her head, knew she was saying "No, no, no" in that muted, hateful whine that echoed off the inside of her skull.

He was strong enough to uncurl her, so she was braced to lose, panic threatening to make her hyperventilate. But he settled next to her. His fingers caressed her ear, her nape, a soothing stroke. Once, twice...until nerve endings stopped cowering and reached for his touch instead. Then his lips were there, teasing flesh that had not forgotten that wonderful, free-fall feeling of arousal, those nerves strumming to life. He reclined on his hip behind her, his large hand stroking down the length of her thigh, his denim-covered groin cradling her bare ass. She stayed still, barely breathing, a rabbit hiding as he went down to her knee, then back up, tracing the curve of buttock as she quivered and a breath escaped her.

She hadn't been touched by anyone but doctors and nurses for months. They examined, poked, prodded. Even though they made every effort to put her at ease, to be gentle, it was always as if they came from every direction, like an enemy attack. She refused to go back to the therapy sessions to learn "how to be blind." She pretty much had a grasp of it. It sucked, and since she could barely hear what most people said to her, being around people at all was exhausting. She'd stopped paying attention. The dark void was quiet and dull, and attempts to draw her out of it made her angry and vicious, as she'd just demonstrated in such an embarrassing way. When she couldn't see or hear people's reactions, she'd found she didn't give a rat's ass if she pissed them off or hurt their feelings.

Peter's every emotional reaction was physical and immediate. And they mattered to her, damn it. Whatever decibel he was using, she could hear him without strain. It was good but frustrating as well. He wasn't going to be ignored.

Curling into a ball had not been a well-thought-out plan, either, for his fingers followed the curve of her buttock to her pussy, teasing the petals with gentle, light but inexorable fingers.

"Peter..." She couldn't help the whimper, the tears that squeezed out at being touched in such an intimate way, after everything else. If her body aroused like a normal healthy woman's, when she was anything but, she might shatter. "I can't bear it."

"Shh...let me hold you. I've burned to hold you, sweetheart."

His other arm tunneled beneath her, wrapping around her chest so she automatically latched her hands onto his forearm. Because of that, he brought her fetal-curved body farther into the shelter of his body. But he changed that altogether paternal image when he collared her throat with a large hand, forcing her head up and back against his shoulder.

Every nerve ending detonated, and not merely the physical ones. Damn him for knowing a submissive's mind too well. The shudder went all the way from that point of contact to her toes, and her thighs loosened a little more. His fingers dipped in, found moisture and spread it over those lips like honey. She mewled, gasped some more. "You won't call me by my name without permission. You know who I am. Tell me."

She couldn't call him Master. She wasn't that person anymore, couldn't pretend she was. Whatever this moment was, he deserved better, more, and that was a road she could no longer travel with him. She had nothing to give. So she shook her head against his hold, even though she couldn't change the thundering of her heart, the aching hardness of her nipples, needing his mouth and touch, the ruthless tug of his fingers. Ah, God, she'd thought a million times about the things he'd done to her breasts.

Two fingers entered her pussy, stroked, thrust. One leg shifted over hers, keeping her legs in their folded position, thwarting her desire to open them. His thumb passed over her clit again and she cried out. She wanted to fight this, wanted to shut everything down, shut him out, but he wasn't letting her. If she could shut down her emotions, maybe she'd dare to perform like a whore in truth. He'd know, and be pissed off enough to leave her alone. But she couldn't.

Every good thing she'd had in the past months had revolved around thoughts of that night, of those letters Dana had long ago committed to memory.

Even though I'd love to hear your sweet voice, even if it was only words on a page, it doesn't matter. When I sleep, I share dreams with you. You're right next to me in this cot. I hear your breathing, and feel peace; at the same time I ache because you're also so far away. I think loving you, having you in my life, will be like that. A never-ending craving and peace at once.

. . .

59

"Dana, say it."

She shook her head again. She couldn't give herself that dream. Not for real.

He rolled her to her back. She clutched the shirt, but she'd defended the wrong perimeter. Putting her legs over his shoulders, he knelt and put his mouth between her legs.

The minute those clever lips touched her pussy, she bowed up, nearly swallowing her tongue. After the surgeries and healing of her physical injuries, there'd been no extremes of pain or pleasure, everything a straight, monotonous highway, the unrelenting fires of hell her mental horizon. This was cold water in desert heat, a miracle and painful shock at once, potentially dangerous if taken too fast or at too extreme a temperature.

He seized her wrists, held them to her sides. *Stop, stop, stop.* Those bottled emotions were rising so fast, the pressure capable of detonating within the sexual response, tearing her apart from the inside. She'd be incapable of distinguishing the emotional torment from the physical. But his tongue knew how to drive thought away. He scraped and teased her cunt, plunged his tongue deep, sucked on her labia, rubbed his face against her so she felt the five-o'clock stubble on her tender inner thighs and the prickle against her sex as he made wide circles, then tight ones, licked and bit.

Her body couldn't care less about the turmoil in her mind. She worked herself against his mouth now, her fingernails digging into his wrists. "Oh, God..."

Her body strained for that pinnacle like an out-of-shape runner. Helping or torturing her, he slowed the pace, lapping at her like a wolf tasting blood, learning her particular flavor. Her foot pressed into his back, heel sliding over the muscled skin beneath his shirt. She thought of the fountain and how he'd laid her on the grass, placing his bare body on hers, the blissful artistry of skin and muscle.

Peter... The sad mental cry of loss washed down the tunnel of memory, a flood of anguish wrenched from deep inside of her. The orgasm turned it into a powerful, mind-shattering force, ripping a scream from her throat. She fought against him, fought the climax. Lost. It took her anyway, put over that edge.

She needed to get free. It was too much and she couldn't handle any more. No more...

When his hands left her at last, the aftershocks were shuddering through her in small jerks. As she went back into a protective ball, rocking, he curled around her again, but this time to hold her tightly. His legs came up under hers, his wide back curved around her, so she was a sea creature safely ensconced in its shell. His breath against her ear became the sound of the ocean, a soft rush that carried her wherever it would. He was stroking her head, a firm, reassuring touch, slow and massaging at once, his thumb caressing the sensitive occipital bone.

"That's it. Let it out."

It was different when someone was holding you, when you mattered specifically to them, not a faceless nurse or VA volunteer being painfully kind. It offered a terrifying glimpse of new possibilities. She couldn't depend on him this way.

That was, unless he didn't give her any other choice. For the first time in months, that thought—not having control—didn't bring bowel-loosening fear. In fact, the kind of anxiety that gripped her now dared to include an emotion she hadn't felt in a while.

Hope.

CHAPTER SEVEN

$\mathcal{P}$eter set Dana's suitcase outside the screen door, with a defining smack intended to catch her attention. It did, her head tilting in response. She was backed up into the corner formed by the entertainment center in her front room, her feet braced. He studied her, the set of the chin, the faint quiver in the hands she clenched against herself.

All it had taken was the idea of leaving this hole and she was back in panic mode, digging in. He'd already seen enough to know he wasn't going to get her to agree to anything by morning. But he'd also seen she still had fight and spirit in her, and knew in his gut the most important thing was to get her out of this bleak cave. Even if he had to take her right now, in the middle of night, when Christina was sleeping. He'd written a note and left it on the front table, so the nurse wouldn't call the cops. Hopefully.

"I'm not going with you, Peter," Dana said. Her voice was one octave away from shrill. "I have no interest in being your little project. I'm fine here, doing just fine."

Yeah, if her life's ambition was to be a mushroom.

When he heard her voice break, saw her too-cold hands grip themselves, he fought his protective instincts for patience. Control. When she'd gripped the hem of her sweatshirt, not wanting him to see what was beneath it, that had been bad enough, but when he stripped off her sweatpants he'd seen the left leg. The scar tissue so twisted and virulent, from knee up to her thigh, a few pings on her shin. And the way she'd shaken under his touch, wanting touch so desperately, but so afraid of it, too, feeling everything he touched as if she was reliving it again.

The longer he stayed quiet now, the more her hands shook. It was epidemic, sweeping through her body. As he approached, she tensed, shrank back against the television. She could feel the floor's vibration, or had detected his scent, his heat. Putting his palms on either side of her, he intensified it.

"Just go away, Peter. Please. Please don't do this to me. Don't destroy that good memory of our night together with some pathetic attempt to pretend there can be more now. Maybe there couldn't ever have been. I mean, what do we have in common, really? Except sex."

He leaned in. "Look up at me."

"I can't see you. What's the point?"

"Because I told you to do it. And because you can feel what's coming off of me. You know what's in my eyes, Dana. What do we have in common? Maybe not much. Hell, my mother was a Yale graduate, and my dad was a Texas roughneck, working rigs out in the ocean. When they died, when I was fifteen, they were as crazy in love as ever. People aren't jigsaw puzzles, Dana. Sometimes people don't fit until they rub up against each other, chisel the rough edges and the shields away. The more they want it to work, the more willing they are to do that rubbing."

She tightened her arms across herself. "I don't want to try, Peter. I don't want anything. I just want you to go."

He stared down into her face; then he nodded, straightened. "Okay. I'll just do one more thing." He went to the front door, found what he was looking for and returned. Moving to the side table by the couch, he flipped open the top of the decorative box so it clattered loudly against the cheap wood.

Dana's head went up. "What are you doing?"

"I'm burning these letters. You don't want anything, so they don't mean anything, right? I mean, if what's in them isn't strong enough to weather one of us getting hurt, what's the point? Hell, I guess I'm glad it wasn't me who got blown up, because you would have ditched my ass in a heartbeat."

"Peter, we don't have a relationship. I'm not going to tie you to me because—"

"You're not going to do anything to me. I came here on my own. If there's any tying to be done, I'm the one who'll be doing it." Lighting the edge of one envelope, he waved it to let the smoke drift her way.

Her face transformed. She hadn't thought he'd do it, obviously, but he hadn't realized she'd charge across the room toward him, a thin scream tearing loose from her throat. She hit the coffee table full throttle, slamming it against the sofa as she stumbled forward.

"*Shit.*" Dropping the paper into the metal ash bucket he'd brought in, he leaped for her, catching her right before she fell onto the glass top. But she twisted, making him follow her down to the floor as she writhed, turning on him like a wild animal.

"Those aren't yours. You can't burn them. *Stop.*" She scrambled to her feet, trying to fight past him, trying to get to them, even though she was facing a different direction, disoriented. The expression on her face was horrific. Twisted, desolate, enraged. Hanging on grimly and praying Christina was a heavy sleeper, he raised his voice to catch Dana's attention.

"Dana, settle down. I didn't burn them. They're fine. Listen to me, damn it."

She stopped, panting, her clawed fingers clutching his arms, her muscles still banded in full resistance. She was so weak, though. Her attempts to push against him were comparable to village kids he'd playfully wrestled in Afghanistan. The thought snapped his control and he brought her to her back on the carpet, looming over her.

"I burned some blank stationery Christina left on the table. But goddamn it, I will not leave you here. I don't care if I have to fucking carry you, kicking and screaming, between here and Baton Rouge. I will do it. You're not staying here. This isn't living."

"I don't want to go. Doesn't that matter? Freedom, freedom, freedom. That's my safe word to let me go and *fuck off.*" She snarled it in his face, and then lost it, all those nerves strung tight beneath him spasming as she disintegrated into a full-blown thrashing, screaming tantrum. He had no choice but to pin her full-body, keep his hands cupped behind her head so that she couldn't slam her skull repeatedly against the wood floor. She beat at him, tried to kick, sank her teeth into his shoulder through his T-shirt. Like one of those terriers he'd written her about. Small, tough and honest.

She was broken into a hundred pieces, and couldn't see to pick any of them up. But he could see every one of them. He *would* figure out how to bring them back together. Pressing his face into the side of her head, he squeezed his lids tight, not wanting to let unmanly tears fall when her screams became sobs, a keening wail of pain.

He expected Christina to burst in, but when she didn't, he remembered her words. *She's angry. A lot.* This wasn't the first meltdown she'd heard. It made him relieved and furious at once. He pushed the latter aside with effort.

"It's all right," he said roughly. "I've got you. I'm not letting you go."

"You can't... I'm already gone."

"No, you're not, damn it." He fished for something, anything. "I asked you a question at the end of every one of those letters. You remember?"

It took a while, but at last she nodded. When he warily lifted some of his weight off her, her nose was running. She worked her hand up underneath the weight of him to wipe at it gracelessly, her eyes still streaming in silent anguish. He swallowed.

"I asked you if you'd ever thought about a different career, other than the army. What was your answer to that?"

She sniffled, shook her head. "I...I can't do that anymore."

"What was it?" He wouldn't reassure her yet. If it was something that required sight and full hearing, well, they'd figure out something else she could do and love.

She squeezed her eyes shut, as if she could still see, another way she could hide. "I wanted to be a minister. Give people...faith, and hope, that life could be better."

He stared down at her as the tears increased. She turned her face to the carpet to let the sobs take her anew. Setting his jaw, Peter rose and lifted her off the carpet in one motion.

"We're going," he said.

~

"You owe me such an astronomical favor, I could demand your firstborn. I've met Middle Eastern terrorist leaders less intimidating than that nurse friend of yours. She agreed to three days before calling the cops, but only because I said you'd call her with progress reports and let her talk to Dana whenever she wanted to. She said either way she's going to have a piece of your hide for reneging on your original agreement."

"Dana wouldn't agree to go with me, but she refused for the wrong reason. She doesn't think she deserves me."

"Smart girl. No decent human being deserves you."

Peter offered a suitable hand gesture, which Ben returned, the videoconferencing connection making it a slow-motion movement. The signal at his bayou home was a little broken up at times. Then Ben shrugged. "Seriously, I think you're okay. Christina knows you're good folk. In fact, between you and me, I think she actually expected you to do something like this. Did Jon make the changes you wanted before you got home?"

"Yeah. I've got to go. Give Christina my cell number so she can call me anytime."

"Will do. We still on for tomorrow night?" Ben lifted a brow at Peter's pause. "You rethinking this?"

"Yes. No. Hell, it's been a stressful few hours. Haven't slept since yesterday. Getting an unwilling woman on a flight, even a private one, is a bitch."

"Get some rest," Ben advised, studying him in a way that told Peter he saw that the exhaustion was more than physical. "When you need someone to spell you, give us a buzz. If she'd be more comfortable with a woman, Savannah and Cass are more than willing to take a shift. Good luck."

Peter nodded and cut the line, returning to his living room to face his mutinous houseguest. Her unreasoning rage from hours before had morphed into a woman's silent anger. He wanted to interpret it as an improvement, now more about not wanting to be told what to do, rather than a complete unwillingness to believe there was a good reason to be here.

Fortunately, she'd worn herself out by the time he'd put her in his car, belting her in. They'd been almost to the airport when she rallied. Getting her out of the rental had been a bit of a scuffle, alarming the attendant. Dana informed him that Peter was a complete overbearing bastard, but then thankfully subsided without a demand for police intervention. The attendant had given him an askance look, to which Peter gave him a bland "you know women" look that earned a grin and forward progress.

It gave him hope that, deep inside, she did want to come here. Of course, she'd been scared shitless and he was her only familiar link. As angry as she was, she clung to his side, shaking as he took the shuttle to the private hangar. He described everything as they went, told her what was going to happen before it happened. While she didn't respond, her fingers held on to his as though she were hanging off the side of a cliff. Fuck, had she been out of that house at *all*?

She'd fallen asleep on the plane. While part of it was emotional exhaustion, he knew it was more than that. Ben wasn't the only K&A man he owed. He made a mental note to send Lucas a case of his favorite Scotch. The CFO was a master at pleasuring women with his mouth. The techniques he'd shared with Peter, in a variety of memorable past experiences, were what had sent Dana into that spinning pleasure, which likely had knocked her off balance enough for him to get this far.

He'd carried her to the K&A limo that had met them at their private hangar in Baton Rouge. When she woke in his lap, she'd kept her cheek pressed to his chest. He'd seen the slow movement of her lashes as she blinked. They'd been thick and lustrous that night long ago. He wondered if the injuries made them thinner and more delicate-looking now, or she'd had on more mascara than he'd realized. He'd touched those tiny hairs with his fingers, stroked them. While the car drove toward the outskirts of Baton Rouge, he thought about all the things he wanted to know about her, to give her.

When they reached his house, he'd guided her through the basic landmarks of the different rooms, then settled her in a chair in the main room as he called Ben. She'd remained there, unmoving, her face telling him nothing, though he sensed a cauldron brewing.

He could deal with that. What he couldn't accept was leaving her there another minute. Every tear she'd shed after her climax, the storm of emotion it and his misguided attempt to burn the letters had unleashed, had felt like acid on his insides. He was responsive to women's tears, yes, but this woman affected him differently. She had that first night, and she did now. The vicious pounding in his head was unrelenting. As unreasonable as he knew it was, he should have been there to protect her. He hadn't been, so he was going to help her now.

Despite what she thought, it wasn't charity. He needed to see that fire in her eyes again, see the courage that came with her submission to him, that willingness to surrender that was a gift, not a defeat. She'd dreamed of him for months, she'd said so, while he'd been haunted by her. She haunted him even now, the ghost of a woman hovering over the shell she'd become.

"I'm thirsty," she said abruptly. "Do I have to beg for food and water?"

"I might make you beg for everything. If I remember correctly, the way you begged had a sweet sound to it."

She pressed those luscious lips together, but he saw her swallow. There were women who were submissives only within the defined boundaries of a sexual situation, but for some that craving could touch on a wide variety of things, and he knew she was one of them. That would help here. He knew it, if he could figure out how to tip the scales away from her fears. He was banking on the fact her passion for life would be inextricably tangled with the desires of the flesh. And her response earlier said she hadn't yet cut those ties, thank God.

While he'd been content to be a Dom within other women's boundaries, this was the kind of submissive he'd wanted. One who had that tantalizing undercurrent. Savannah and Cass were similar, another way the K&A men were alike in their needs and desires. When Jon and Ben found their own women, he'd lay money it would be the same.

He went to a squat by the straight chair in which she sat so rigid, wearing the baggy jeans he'd put on under her sweatshirt. He'd left most of her clothes there, because he wanted her to leave that persona behind. As soon as he could get her out of these, he'd probably burn them.

"If you're hungry or thirsty, Dana"—he traced her lips with a forefinger—"ask your Master for food and something to drink."

That same painful and rigid expression crossed her face. "Peter, please don't. I'm feeling too vulnerable right now, you know?"

"I know. But here's the deal, sweetheart." He shifted so his splayed knees were bracketing her calves. His one hand closed over both of hers, clenched in her lap. "Give me three days. Be what you would have wanted to be to me, and trust me to help you do that. On day three, if you want to go back to that damn box, I'll take you there myself. But give me that. What do you have to lose?"

He was lying, of course. Even when K&A did their negotiations, he was the floor man, the guy who went in and evaluated a plant's assets and their production processes. He wasn't the poker player like the others. But he put everything into his voice to convince her he meant it, that he would take her back to that pointless existence if he couldn't get through to her. Even though she had no one else.

Yeah, right.

There were times that lying in a relationship was the best thing. He had no qualms that this was one of those moments, whether he was lying to her or she was lying to herself about believing him. But in the space of a held breath, she gave a short, barely there nod. "Okay," she whispered.

~

Dana felt his hand tighten over hers, an approval. She knew this was wrong, but he'd brought her here, his will irresistible. How was she going to say no in three days, when she couldn't say no now? And why *wasn't* she saying no? Was it a pathetic reason, letting her destiny be decided like a broken branch carried by whitewater? Or was there a kernel of hope left inside of her, a hope that some will to live that had escaped her these many months still existed in her heart and soul, and he could find it? She didn't know. But for now, she'd made her decision. She'd be that broken branch and see where she ended up, as long as she didn't take him over the falls with her. She was just afraid that she wouldn't care, that she'd cling to him so she wouldn't fall alone. And she'd never been pathetic like that.

"All right." His fingers caressed her palm. "Let me show you a few more things."

He rose, and drew her up with him. She didn't like being in unfamiliar surroundings, but with his arm around her waist, guiding her, she tried to relax, somehow knowing he wouldn't let her stumble over things. "What's that scent?"

"Jasmine, from my front yard. Jon had some cut. Mixed with

lavender." He guided her to the pottery vase that held them, molded her palms over it. There were smooth rolls, curves, not like a normal bulb vase. She took over the investigation, her brow furrowing as she worked her way up it, then sideways, and back up again, until she found the flowers, the thin stems and nodding blossoms. He had a fan going, and they were swaying in the faint breeze. He had a screen open as well, because she could hear shrill birds crying out over what he said was the bayou. She could smell it, the damp vegetation and salt.

"It's a person, isn't it? The vase."

He closed his hands over hers, leading her to the clay features, distracting her with the brush of his fingers on her knuckles. "It's an abstract reclining nude. She's lying on her hip, her hands folded under her face. Her skin is texturized like a tree's bark, the flowers forming the canopy." He paused. "It's a piece by a famous local Louisiana artist. The finish is ebony. Jon bought it while I was away. Thought I'd like it."

"Oh, yeah? You got a thing for black girls, Captain?"

"Lately. One in particular." He caressed the sensitive bone of her forefinger, his intent obviously sensual. Dana swallowed, her touch spasming against the curve of the sculpture's head and slim neck.

"He didn't include hair."

"No. The artist wanted the beautiful line of her skull. Long hair would interfere with that." He touched her ear with his other hand, moved to the erogenous zone at the base of her own skull, massaging, slow. "If you decide to stay, I'll take you to some of the galleries here. I bet you can give me a different perspective on the pieces."

She stiffened, drew back. "Sure. I'll write up reviews for the local paper. Don't give me the blindness-heightens-your-other-senses bullshit."

"The fact it pisses you off doesn't make it less true. As responsive as you were that first night, I can tell that you're hypersensitive to every inch I move over your skin now. And you want more of it, are about to go crazy for it. I know I am."

There was no boast, simply quiet fact. She folded her arms over her chest, but she wanted to move away, and couldn't do that without using her arms. As much as she knew he wouldn't let her fall or run into anything, it was an instinct when she couldn't see. So she dropped them with an annoyed sigh and moved away from him. Her thigh pressed the edge of an easy chair, and when she glided her fingers along it, she found something even softer than the cushioning. And furry. She lifted it to her face. "A stuffed animal?"

"A kitten. It was a housewarming gift from Ben when I moved in." He cleared his throat. "Said if I moved out into the sticks, it was the only pussy I'd get out here."

"He cares about you." The wary smile tickled her cheeks, muscles she hadn't used in a while. "He's not harboring some secret lust for you, right?"

Peter snorted. "If I was the last fuckable thing in the universe, and then only because he has to stick his cock into something every twenty-four hours or he thinks it will self-destruct. If it came to that, I'd break it off for him."

"You love him, too," she realized. She moved on before he could reply, trailing her fingers along the silky surface of an end table. A tall house plant, a palm, brushed her face with scratchy edges. The walls she touched to the right of the open window were beadboard, the drapes a clean-smelling cotton. As she made her way around his living room, she noted he didn't have enormous amounts of furniture, but what he did have held a plethora of objects to discover. At one small table there was a chess game. In process, if the positioning of the pieces were any indication. Her brow furrowed again. "This isn't a traditional set. It's pewter, and the figures are..."

"Toy soldiers. That one was Lucas's gift. They all look really GI Joe–ish. Except the Queen figure is Barbie. Carrying an M-16." There was a smile in his voice. "It's an older set."

"They're your family. The men you work with." She knew them from his letters. He'd talked about them frequently there.

"Yes. Once you decide someone's your family, you watch after each other." He let it hang there, the significance obvious. Since Dana didn't know what to say to such an absurd implication, she kept moving, but she knew she was orbiting around his scent and heat, keeping him close. He was right about the hypersensitivity. Those few inches of her flesh he'd brushed with his were still tingling.

It had been so long since she'd reached out to explore her surroundings, as if she were a scared, lost camper who couldn't appreciate the woods, preferring to huddle over the fire and stare down at the small tin of provisions she had left. But in his presence, where she felt absurdly safe, she was absorbing smells, seeking to touch, to recognize things. She'd been cold a lot, but now she was warm in the sweatshirt. The room apparently received plenty of sun, so it must have west-facing windows, given the time of day. If she could see, she imagined she would be bathed in light.

What the hell was the matter with her? She should be majorly pissed off, keeping her ass in that chair until he took her back. But that last tantrum had been her worst yet, and they'd been occurring more frequently lately, as if her body were screaming to split away from her damaged soul, get out and run, blindness or no blindness. She couldn't deny it felt...different to be somewhere new, somewhere not about herself.

"Can I borrow a T-shirt?" she said, trying to hold on to her sullen tone. "Or did your loyal minions arrange for me to have a wardrobe?"

"The idea of keeping you naked is appealing, but they did actually bring some things by. Let's get you a shower first."

The image of him compelling her to stay in his home without anything to warm her but himself was distracting. But when his hands settled on the hem of her shirt again, she automatically latched onto his wrists to hold it down.

She could feel the weight of his stare in the silence. "Let go of me, Dana."

She knew that voice. Even with her degraded hearing, she knew the sound of a Master taking command. From the second he'd come to her place, he'd been proceeding under the assumption she desired that, even outside of a club. Like so many other things, he was right, before even she'd realized how much. She hadn't ever indulged it that way, not trusting any Master enough. Before her accident, she'd wanted to do so, enough that her skin rippled with gooseflesh at the sound of it now. The idea had been terrifying to her then. While she was surprised at how little fear she had of relinquishing herself into his hands, when she had so little control to relinquish, she still couldn't release him, because of other fears.

"I'm afraid of what you'll see." The rawness of it resounded in her head.

"You don't have to be afraid of anything with me." The steel was still there, but as implacable tenderness. "Lift your arms."

Slowly, she released her hold, one finger at a time. When she lifted trembling arms above her head, he pulled the sweatshirt free.

She hadn't been wearing a bra, so moist marsh air touched her bare flesh, making her nipples peak. He opened the jeans he'd had her don at the duplex, made her step out of her shoes, then stripped them off with her panties, leaving her completely naked.

The scar tissue marked the left side of her torso and leg like a crazy quilt design. Sick of dealing with doctors, she hadn't scheduled any more cosmetic surgery since her face. At the time she made that decision, she didn't care about how she looked. Now she desperately wished she'd done it. She supposed Peter would consider that progress, but resentment and terror warred inside of her at his lack of immediate response.

He'd settled his hands on her upper arms, keeping her squarely facing him. His breath was slow, steady. Too slow and steady. Something about it suggested...barely suppressed anger. His palms were heating with it. Part of her was intimidated, another part enthralled by the dangerous power of him, so near. He was angry at faceless enemies, she realized, at someone who would dare hurt her, leave her looking like a toy someone had broken and should have cast away.

His finger traced the mark beneath her left breast. "Does any of it hurt?"

"Not really. The ribs and arm hurt some when it gets too cold, but the scars don't hurt anymore." At least not the way he meant. She was pathetic. There were people far worse off than her. She should be able to handle this, but all she wanted to do when she thought about it, touched it, was cry like a little girl over what she'd lost. She'd had pretty, unblemished skin. She'd liked the line of her hip, the smooth roundness of her shoulder, the unmarked perfection of her left breast. While she couldn't see it, she could feel it, the rough texture.

Maybe that was why the "heightened senses" platitude made her so angry. Heightened senses could be a curse, because she could feel every scar like the surface of the moon. She told herself to be glad she didn't have eyes to confirm it. Though she'd never see the wide, wide ocean again. Or Peter's smile.

"Please speak. If you don't speak, I'm going to lose my mind."

"I'm looking at a beautiful, brave and foolish woman. One I'm very, very glad is alive."

CHAPTER EIGHT

*S*he bit her lip, overcome, but he didn't require her words. He reached away from her, and she heard the slide of something like metal across a table surface. When he brought it up, it brushed her sternum. Jewelry. Or... Her heart rate started accelerating.

As he put the collar on her throat, she followed it there, passing her fingers over his wrist, then down to the wide strap, lined so it wouldn't chafe. A waterfall of decorative chains fell from it. It had a D-ring loop, with a pendant. Touching the oblong disk, she realized it was a medallion. Because she'd replayed every detail she remembered about him that night, her throat closed, already knowing.

"It's the St. Christopher's I wear." He increased the collar's constriction, resulting in a violent contraction low in her belly. Her fingers trembled where they rested on his thick wrist. "You know the rules, Dana. While you wear this, I'm your Master. You're mine. You follow my orders; you do what I tell you."

"But I didn't... I refused to call you that."

He touched her chin, lifted her face, and she sensed him so close, the idea of his mouth hovering so near overwhelming her. "Are you going to refuse now?" he asked.

She swallowed. A hundred denials leaped to mind, but it wasn't her rational mind running things now. "No."

"No, what?" His tone sharpened, making her jump. She responded automatically, pushing all worries and concerns aside.

HONOR BOUND

"No, Master."

"Good." The deep pleasure in his voice rippled through her. "Because we have some business to handle before I bathe and dress you the way I want."

Taking her arm, he guided her back toward the main source of that marsh breeze. She heard the creak of a screen door opening, and he was leading her out before she could balk.

She hated it, but her legs started to tremble. The give of the boards suggested she was being led onto a boat dock. That meant they were surrounded by water, and she was completely naked. One misstep, and she'd be in the water. Her fingers crept up to hold his hand at her waist, knuckles burrowing into his palm. She was thankful he didn't admonish her for lack of trust, but squeezed that hand, reassuring her without words.

She started when something dragged against her skin. Before she could panic, he stopped, guided her hand to touch long, waving grass. It apparently grew up along the sides of this part of the dock, tall enough to tease her bare ankles. As the strands moved under her palm, she took a deep breath, focused on their motion. Her nostrils flared, bringing her the aroma secreted in their sun-soaked stalks and darker, moist places near the waterline.

"The smell is so vivid, you can almost see it, can't you? C'mon. I want to take you to the end of the dock."

When she straightened, he led her onward, no hesitation, a smooth pace that had her stomach jumping like the frogs she could faintly hear croaking, which meant they were making quite a racket near the dock. At the end, he let her feel the edge with her toes, then put her hands on a piling. The wood had a worn texture under her palms.

"Now, if I vanished all of a sudden"—he stroked a hand along her tense shoulder—"which is *not* going to happen, there's one of these every five feet or so, and a rope runs between them. If you want to come out here, you can follow that rope, sit on these boards, get some sun. When you reach this one"—his grip increased over hers—"you'll know it's the end, because there's a knot to the rope." He showed her that, his fingers sure on hers. "Below that is the water, and my boat. I'll take you out on it soon."

"Great. I'll probably get seasick." She was having trouble enough

75

walking on solid surfaces. She wasn't sure she wanted to think about the unstable glide of a boat.

"It's a smooth, easy ride. I paddle it most times. A lot of nights, I sit out here and drink a beer after work. Listen to the frogs, all the night sounds, until the bugs outnumber my zappers and drive me back into the screened porch."

She yelped as something ice-cold touched her, and he caught her waist before she instinctively leaped right, which would have taken her into the water. She grabbed his biceps anyway, cursing him. He chuckled. "Language, sweetheart. It's a beer. There's an outdoor mini fridge here. Want a sip of mine?"

She tried to draw a steadying breath, wondering if she was the only one who realized she was completely naked in broad daylight. "Not going to offer me one?"

His hand, cool and wet from the beer's condensation, drew a line down the outer curve of her breast, slow and easy. "No. You'll drink from mine, if you ask nice."

Yeah, he knew she was naked. As flustered as she was, she detected full awareness of it in the sexy intensity of his voice. "But first, we're going to get that business out of the way I was talking about."

He shifted to set down the beer, then straightened to bring both her hands up to the piling. Looping a coil of line around her wrists, he guided her hands to a metal hook embedded in the piling before he drew up the slack, locking her wrists against it.

Well, at least if she was tied here, she couldn't fall into the water. But her breath was still getting short, the restraint doing funny things to her insides, anticipating what he was planning.

"I'm not sure I'm ready for this."

He slid his hand down her arm to her back, to the curve of her buttock. Then, as he had the night in the club, without preamble or permission, he eased his fingers between her legs. She gasped as he stroked the wetness there, brought it back out and painted the moisture over her sex before he took her hand to his mouth, let her feel him taste his own fingers, a quick swipe of his tongue. "You're ready, Sergeant. Now, I gave you one clear order when you left. What was it? You'd better remember it."

A few hours ago, she'd been huddled in a dark room. In a way that didn't ignore or minimize her physical limitations, he was nevertheless acting as though they had no bearing on how he intended their relationship to progress, as if she'd returned whole and wanted to try out a 24/7 Master/sub relationship with him.

Holy God. She yelped as a strip of heat sizzled down her backside. The switch.

"Yep." His voice held dark satisfaction, a thick stew of lust. "Liked the results so much last time, decided to get my own. Answer me quick, Sergeant."

"You told me to keep my ass down, sir."

"And did you?"

"No, sir."

"There are a couple soldiers who likely wouldn't be alive if you had. You did your duty as a soldier, but you overrode your Master's command. You did right, but you still have to be punished, don't you?"

"Yes, Master." Her fingers gripped the post, her mind whirling. "How many lashes do you think you deserve for risking what belongs to me?"

She swallowed again, feeling a fear different from any she'd felt in the past long months, fear wrapped up in building need. Slick arousal was trickling down her thigh.

"Five," she stammered out, sensing that hand getting ready to flick again. With his strength, she didn't think she'd last more than five before screaming her lungs out. How close was the nearest neighbor?

"Really? Hmm." He shifted to her other side, and when his hand ran down her flank, she jumped, anticipating the switch. "I'll ask you the question again, after I give you the five *you* prefer."

Oh, son of a bitch. She was wrong. Not only in her answer, but in how many stripes of that branch she could take without screaming. Her skin was tender from too much sitting, too few workouts, and the next one felt like bacon grease in an open wound. Two, three... The cry ripped from her throat, so loud she heard the echo. The faint frog and bird sounds disappeared. He didn't pause. Four and five.

Gasping for breath, she whimpered with shock and relief as he rolled the cold brew over her buttock, slow, easy, taking out the stinging throb. Back and forth, as the hand holding the switch took a firm grip of the other cheek, kneaded it with casual, indulgent pleasure. "It's softer, Sergeant, but it's still a nice ass. Now, you going to try for the *right* answer to that question?"

She nodded. "However many my Master feels I deserve."

"Bingo." He pressed against her back then, and she sucked in a startled breath as the switch bent across her throat, below the collar, hauling her head up against his jaw. He pressed his groin against her aching backside, and he was hard as a rock, making her want to widen her stance. Her nipples ached below that restraint, every reaction she had responding to the demand of his body.

"That suspended second in time, when I didn't know if Jon was going to tell me if you were dead? There aren't enough lashes in the world to make up for that feeling. Then there's not telling me what was happening, not calling for my help. I could stripe your ass bloody in a heartbeat, Sergeant, for those things. I mean that."

"I didn't want you to come to me out of pity, damn it." His anger goaded her pain, her heart wrenched between emotions and lust.

"I would have come because you belonged to me the second you met my gaze at The Zone. Which is why, tomorrow night, you and I are going to visit my local club here. I'm going to remind you of that, open those eyes of yours to what you're more than capable of seeing. If you do that, maybe, finally, you'll be ready to take cautious steps toward embracing a new life for yourself. The way you should have been doing, all these months."

A BDSM club? Was he crazy? With lots of people and noise, and ways to fall and run into things and not know where she was or...

His hand settled on the collar. "You're already worrying. Dana, how long have you been a sexual submissive?"

"Most of my life," she whispered. "I've known about it since high school."

"And like a lot of them, you have trust issues, until the right Master takes you in hand." One of those large hands dropped, squeezed a sore buttock again, earning a gasp. "Between now and tomorrow, you'll feel better about that. You're going to serve me the way a slave should. I'm going to keep you hot and wanting, all day long. You're going to talk, a lot, and tell me everything going on in that head or heart of yours. You'll trust me with everything. If you hold anything back, if I suspect at any time you're hiding anything from me, I bring you back out here, and we go again. Believe me, I'm pissed enough to take pleasure in beating your ass a few more times."

She heard the rough emotion under the hard words. He was controlled, but that roughness, what it implied, was harder to face than a hundred more times at his whipping post. She didn't want to care how he felt. She'd kept herself walled up, feeling as if she'd fucking tear the world apart if she let loose, but he was strong. Maybe tougher than her. Right? He could handle it. But that itself was too damn appealing, too fast.

She rested her temple against the piling, fingers digging in again. "What will it change?" she asked, unable to keep the bitterness out of her voice.

His hand slid around her front, cupping her hip bone. When his tone softened, she choked on a sob. "Why don't we see?" he said. "I know you're scared about tomorrow night. But I'm going to have a gift for you, something that will help you embrace your own pleasure without fear. I promise. So I don't want you to worry about that, about anything. Okay? Can you do that for your Master? Will you trust me that much?"

I want to. Oh, how easy he made it sound, and yet she felt as if he'd put her on a roller coaster before she was ready to go to dizzying heights at such speeds. But there was an amazing, small part of her mind that didn't want to cower, a burning light that made her summon up a scrap of courage, and speak. "You said something about a sip of your beer?"

He gave it to her with her hands still tied, so she had to lay her head in the cup of his palm, trust him to guide the fluid into her mouth. As she swallowed, he stroked her throat, then down over her sternum, teasing the tops of her breasts as if he saw no scar tissue at all. They didn't behave as if they were anything less than they'd always been, nerves awakening under his hands, the curves swelling and nipples hardening further.

When he finally released her from the hook, he took her back to the bench, keeping her hands tied. As he sat down, holding her between his knees, she imagined how he looked there, in a pair of jeans fitting just right, maybe his arm stretched across the bench. She could sit down next to him, or on that knee, but her mind turned to what she'd almost done in the apartment, the way she'd gone to her knees. She'd been goaded by darker feelings then, but now…

She realized she was trailing one of the fingers of her bound hands along his knee, a two- or three-inch stretch, a nervous movement back and forth.

"My slave appears to know what I like best with my evening beer."

His voice was husky, and she quivered at the sound of a loosened belt buckle hitting the bench, imagining the purr of a zipper. She envisioned his cock stretching up in all its hard, thick glory, him leaning back against the rail, sipping the beer as she serviced him with her mouth. That organ glistening with her saliva, her ass red with his punishment. Her knees were already folding beneath her, without conscious direction. His hands were there, though, guiding her down, and he held her weight until he'd put a cushion on the boards for her knees. His touch lingered on her nape as both sets of her fingers crept up his inner thighs, accommodating her tied wrists.

She hadn't had the opportunity to touch him much that first night, or even last night. Now he indulged her pace, letting her explore the texture of the light mat of hair on his muscled thighs, the smooth flesh of the insides, the encroaching heat of his groin as she drew closer to his testicles, working her way to what she knew awaited her.

When her hand closed greedily over the hot, hard base, she felt him suck in a breath, a gratifying one. Dominance and submission were all about power and control, a perfect state of trust and surrender. By taking away so many of her decisions right now, Peter was giving her the chance to fully evaluate the one decision that would be hers to make when three days were over.

Before her injury, she'd wanted that perfect state handed to her on a platter. Ironically, blindness and Peter's arrival had shown her the devastating truth. It was a leap of faith. Had she lost her ability to leap that far, though? How could she even know the right direction to leap when she couldn't see him, couldn't hear the sound of his heart calling to hers?

"Shh. Stop thinking."

The reassurance and warning in his tone returned her attention to the weight of him in her hand. Heated, silken skin over steel, the musky, aroused aroma as she brought her mouth down, stretched her lips over the broad head, tasted the salt of him, fluid already gathered on the tip.

He stroked the shell of her ear that had the hearing aid. He didn't dislodge it, the movement easy and familiar, not the exaggerated care that would have distracted her. It brought her back to thinking about what had changed since they'd last seen each other. And yet, she liked it when his fingers convulsed abruptly as she went down, relaxing her throat to take him deep. Skills that didn't rely on her sight and hearing were enhanced by this singular focus on taste and smell, his physical reaction. For the first time, she felt a tiny trickle of satisfaction with the thought. Something within her power to give.

While the idea of him drinking his beer excited her, this casual use of his slave, she also liked the idea of him being too aroused to do anything other than dig in for the ride, so she put all her effort into it.

His thighs trembled, and he thrust up. She scored him with her teeth, swirled her tongue over the base, found his heavy testicle sac and squeezed it, caressing the sensitive perineum. She knew how to slide a finger slow and easy up his backside and make him see stars, but for now she focused on this.

She did miss hearing him, the guttural whispers an aroused Master would make, the murmured command to suck his cock harder, faster. As if he knew that, the clutch of his hand and the thrust of his hips communicated that message, making her wetter. She wanted him between her legs, wanted to feel whole and real. She also craved the spurt of his seed into the back of her throat, his roar of release vibrating through her touch, breaking that muted sound barrier.

When he came, it was all that and more, his hand clenching on the back of her neck, his cock thrusting into her mouth so hard it was all she could do to keep in rhythm, drawing it out as seed flooded her throat and tongue. She heard his male groan of satisfaction, the animal sound of it thrilling her to her toes, her calves slick with her arousal. She didn't slow down until he started twitching with the sensitivity. Licking him, teasing him with small kisses and nips, she savored his shudders. He caught her chin and pulled her up, lifted her in an amazing display of strength to straddle his lap. He kept her off his cock, despite her moan of protest. Instead, he cradled her face and cleaned his fluids from her lips with his T-shirt, wiping the moisture from her eyes, caused by the strain of powerful thrusts. Finding his abdomen beneath the raised cotton, she dug into his muscles with needy fingers.

"God, your cunt is so flushed and swollen. You want your Master to fuck you, don't you?"

When she nodded, he claimed her lips, tasted himself and her at once. He gripped her ass, made her writhe against him, whimper as he prolonged the wet, sucking pleasure of his mouth. But then he drew back and held her, his hand on her throat where the collar was, a reminder. "Not right now, but soon. First, I'm giving you that bath."

She'd tried to protest, explain she did know how to shower herself, but that had won her a stinging swat on the bottom before he shepherded her into the garden tub. He'd given her a very thorough bath, embarrassing and arousing at once. Sliding his fingers into her pussy as well as her rectum, he left her on the cusp of climax before he turned to rinsing her, stimulating her nipples with the sprayer.

God, she wanted him inside her, but the frustrating fact was that she wasn't used to so much physical exertion, and he was far too intuitive. "It's bedtime," he said after he dried her gently, cupped her face. "There'll be time for the rest."

He even carried her to his bedroom, a sign that she couldn't conceal her utter lassitude. It had a quiet, tranquil feel to it, an aroma of wood and Peter. The bed's cushiony quilt and abundance of pillows also bore his reassuring scent. He lay down with her, a consolation prize, and while she lay with her head on his chest, he described everything in the room in detail, from the overflowing bowl of change he had on the dresser, to his pictures, snapshots of his travels for his company and with the military, and the view of the bayou out the open screened window. He did so well she couldn't help but see it all, imagine herself as part of it, him wrapped around her.

When he at last went quiet, probably to give her the chance to doze off, she remembered what he'd said out on the dock. *Tell me everything going on in that head or heart of yours. Trust me with everything.*

"Can I ask you something?"

"You can ask me anything."

She nodded, rubbing the firm pectorals beneath her cheek. Reaching up, she stroked the curve of one, found the bump of his nipple. "Were my tattoos ruined?"

His hand drifted down her back, traced the eagle and flag, then moved to the Lord's Hands. "No. Your promise to your grandmother is still there."

She wondered why it didn't surprise her that he understood the most important one to her. "When I got it, she said only trashy women got tattoos. And she worried that it might be blasphemous. But I think she liked it. She put her palm on it, said a prayer for me. So I've always felt her hand there, too."

"I'm sorry she died, Dana. She sounds like a wonderful woman. Do you think she would have liked me?"

She would have loved him. But for form's sake, Dana sniffed. "She'd have said you need to be taken down a peg or two. But she would have tolerated you."

He chuckled, and the warmth of it slid through her, thickened her throat as she imagined him and Grams together, the banter they would have shared. How gently Peter would have treated her. She sought another subject before tears made her foolish. "Why did you decide to be a soldier? I bet you were an adrenaline junkie."

"It was probably some of that," he admitted. "But eventually I matured enough to realize how damn lucky I am to live here, to be given the blessings I have. So I pay it forward, hoping to give those choices to others. I know how that sounds these days. People make fun of it, think a guy like me is stupid."

"I don't," she said, and he stilled, their hands intertwined. "I hate what happened to me, Peter. But I believed in what I was doing, despite some of the bullshit we deal with. I had a purpose."

But what was her purpose now?

As if sensing her mood trying to slide downward again, he gave her a playful squeeze, shifted to speak closer to her ear, tease her with his breath. "I admit, I throw in the pay-it-forward thing to make me sound sensitive, rather than a macho chauvinist Rambo. Impress the girls."

"I like Rambo." She smiled against his muscular heat, brushed her lips there. "And you've already blown your cover. I know you're a macho chauvinist. Sitting out on your dock, making your woman give you head while you drink beer and watch alligators."

"You passed the audition with flying colors. Most I interview fail miserably, though I give a few of them points for enthusiasm."

She thumped him, but when he caught her fist, the humor had disappeared from his voice, leaving a rough note that told her she wasn't the only one vibrating with need. "My woman. I like the sound of that."

So did she, fool that she was. "You are sensitive, in some ways," she said. *The way a man should be sensitive.* She could hear the reassuring beat of his heart so easily this way, her cheek pressed to his chest. "A little heavy-handed and possessive, but there's nothing mean about you. You're determined, and you believe in what's right and wrong. You'd tear your heart out if someone really needed it." She traced his pectoral again, let her fingers start to drift downward.

"Using flattery to have your way with me?" But despite the teasing, there was a strained quality to his voice.

"I know you're hard, Master. Why won't you fuck your slave?" She made it a whisper and felt the jump under her hand where she'd managed to inch down to his cock, slide it over the head, straining against fabric. He caught her hand.

"Because she's tired, and my first job is to take care of her. So she'll be up for serving my needs later." He brushed his lips across her brow. "Though I'm pleased you're thinking about wanting to please me."

She was. She was also surprised by how urgent her need was to perform that role for him, no matter her exhaustion. Before her accident happened, she'd realized that the night between them had gone far beyond roles and performances. Her need for him, to be his submissive, had only grown fiercer the longer she was away from him. The craving was as relentless now, practically blood and bone deep.

She'd been so quick to believe it was gone, beyond her reach, but a need like this didn't evaporate on command. Every time she'd thought of him or heard one of his letters, it had stirred, but at his reappearance, it had flared high and hot, restored to full, vibrant life. Vibrant anything was something she'd thought beyond her reach as well.

He held her like a velvet cuff, relentless and gentle both, and she relaxed into that hold. When she slid into the warm waters of a dreamless sleep, she was still confused, but for the first time in a long time, she lacked the jagged ache in her throat, the lonely sense of isolation squeezing her heart. He was here, and she could sleep in his arms.

CHAPTER NINE

*S*he didn't wake until the next morning. While the loss of time caused her some chagrin, she was amazed she'd slept so deeply. She woke as she'd fallen asleep, secure in his arms, and wondered if he'd moved at all. His body was warm and strong beneath hers, his thigh still tangled with both of hers, which initiated all sorts of prurient thoughts. He wasn't going to be deterred, however. He pressed a kiss to her temple before she could push for something more, and lifted her out of the bed.

"We'll do a workout, and then have some breakfast. I've got a sports bra and shorts here for you."

The man had a damn Gold's Gym in his house. Within no time, she was sure he must have been a drill sergeant before he was an officer. He put her on his treadmill, guiding her hands to the supports, and then worked her up to some god-awful speed guaranteed to send her into cardiac arrest. Right before that red zone, he put her into cool-down. While she listened to the faint clink and thud of weights as he did his lifting near her, she could smell the pleasant aroma of male sweat, and imagined him there, on his back, lifting the bar over his head.

"How much do you press?" she asked, fumbling for the towel he'd left on the treadmill arm to pat her sweaty neck. Now that she was thinking about it, she realized the speed and incline probably weren't that hard—she was just so damn out of shape.

"Two hundred this morning. I do about four hundred in a dead-weight lift. You did good. Pull the tab out and the treadmill will stop. Then come over here."

A clank and shudder through the floor suggested he'd dropped the weights into their cradle. She stepped off the treadmill, lifted her hands, seeking the weight set or him. She located him, or rather his bare, slick chest. Her fingers drifted, finding from his loose waistband that he was wearing only a pair of jeans. She wondered if he was bare-foot, liking that picture. His short hair maybe a little rumpled, since neither of them had showered yet. Lifting her hand to his face, she traced his jaw, felt the morning shadow. "Is it gold, like your chest?"

"Yeah. Or as Lucas calls it, baby hair."

She smiled. "You know there's an inverse relationship between how much men care about one another and how much they insult one another."

"That's why we have girls. So we can be emotional and wimpy with someone who won't hold it against us."

"Yeah, right. You big pussy."

He chuckled. "Not a good idea to insult your personal trainer this morning. Not if you want pancakes for breakfast."

He took her through the machines and again pushed her to her limits, though she found that severely below where she'd once been. It didn't matter that she'd been part of the cause, unwilling to move out of a chair for months. She couldn't help resenting it, how quickly she exhausted, the weakness of the left side. For some perverse reason, it underscored how handicapped she felt, even though this was some-thing she knew she *could* change. She was biting back tears by the time she worked her way around to all the machines and found she could barely meet the minimum recommended reps.

It didn't make it any easier that he held all the control, holding himself away from her like a damn animated piñata she couldn't see, taunting her with his proximity.

"You're getting there. Here." He guided her hands up to the triceps pull, even though her arms were shaking. "Hold on to these."

"I can't do any more. I'm—"

He closed his hands over hers, holding her grip, but instead of getting tougher with her, he bent to her throat to suck off the beads of sweat gathered in the tender pocket formed by her collarbone, right under her collar. Her rapid breath caught in her throat, and she let out a moan he answered by following the track down to her cleavage. The sports bra was tight, too tight. When he cupped her, she wanted to feel the callused palms against her female flesh. He answered her unspoken desire, pushing up the plastic band and letting it constrict over the curves, baring her nipples to the air.

"Oh, God..." He was fondling her, slow, kneading strokes and pinches of the nipple, as if he had all the time in the world. Her hands convulsed on the pulleys. How did he know to shift his attention from the weight of the curve, to tracing the shape, to teasing the nipple, and alternating the stimulation in myriad delicious ways, making her rock against him, gasp and groan at the torture? He didn't have to say how much he adored her breasts. She felt it in every touch, in his heated attention to every inch of them, but then he spoke, making her crazier.

"I'd love to do breast bondage on you. Use rope to lift and squeeze these beauties, put a bar clamp on them so when I removed it you'd feel tingling through every nerve ending. It'd make you come when the blood rushes back into the nipples. I'd get them pierced so I could keep you in jewels, tug on them whenever I want."

The military didn't allow body piercings. But that wasn't a problem anymore, was it? Though that brought a shot of pain, it was balanced by the image of what he was suggesting. "I bet you like sparkling things, don't you, Dana? I'd put you in diamonds, maybe some gorgeous emeralds, like your eyes."

She tried to use her stomach muscles to lift her legs and wrap them around his hips, but she couldn't do it without his help, and he wouldn't let her get that close. "You want me to touch your pussy so bad, don't you?"

"Please..." she whispered.

"I love your begging, but you don't want it bad enough yet." Adjusting her sports bra back over her breasts, he smoothed his palms over the aching nipples. Before she could say something nasty she was sure would get her into all the right sorts of trouble, he had her doing triceps pulls. Christ. Then hip abductions, the seam of her shorts rubbing against a very wet pussy. But she was using her other senses, and she noted that when he counted off for her, his voice had a tight note. When he went into the next room to get them some more water, the rhythm of his steps through the vibrations of the wood floor was uneven. She curled her lip in feline satisfaction.

"Your gait sounds a little off there, Captain. Hauling something heavy?"

Coming to her side, he helped her find the weight blocks and showed her where to put the pin for the next rep. As he did, he bumped her hip in warning, bouncing her off him a couple feet. "Keep it up, Sergeant."

When she snorted, she heard his sexy, self-deprecating chuckle. "Yeah, yeah, I know. You are. Behave and I'll give you some water."

The bottle had a straw, which he guided to her lips as he drew her close within his arm span. As his palm smoothed over the curve of her ass, he let her rest her hand on his bare chest, though she itched to drop her touch to explore straining denim. "Ready for another rep?"

"No." She suppressed a sigh. "Everything's more difficult. My joints hurt and my balance isn't for shit. I feel like such a damned girl." God, she was whining.

"You are a girl." He gave the back of her head a quick stroke. A soldier's reassurance, not a caress. A brisk gesture that said, *You can do this.* "You know, there's a great yoga person who can help you improve your flexibility and balance. She's a PT as well. We think Jon has the hots for her, so he could charm her into a discount rate."

That should sound like a good idea, but instead it irritated her. She didn't want to go through all this. She just wanted to be herself again, now. She chose not to respond, since she knew she would only sound waspish, but Peter wouldn't let her get away with that. He passed his thumb over her lips. "What're you thinking, sweetheart?"

"I feel like giving up," she confessed after a long moment, the truth of it shuddering through her. "I'm afraid to test my limits, see where they actually are. Maybe it's better not to know. I'm not sure I can handle knowing. I know I'm chickenshit."

She hadn't said things like this to anyone. Maybe not even to herself. Hearing the words resound in her head now made her afraid as well, wanting to take them back. But he kept that gentle stroke going on her face, soothing the scars, the memory of them.

"Yeah, you are a little bit. Hell, anybody would be. But you know what? You could have busted my ass at the car rental place. You didn't. You were brave enough to do this, Dana. I know you felt like it was easier to jump into a firefight with your sight and hearing, knowing who and what you are, than to face the uncertainty of where you're going now, what you can be."

"How would you know that?" she managed.

Pressing his forehead to hers, he cupped her face with both hands as she lifted hers to close on his wrists. "Because it's how I would feel. Only I'd be a lot more scared, because guys always think we have to be the biggest and the strongest."

She stifled a half chuckle, half sob. "Yeah, you called that right." But she kept her forehead pressed to his and, for now, he seemed content to stay there, tracing her ears, letting her get her emotions under control, until she straightened on her own. She set her jaw, moved back to the bench, though it was hard to leave the proximity of those long, clever fingers. "Let's set the pin higher for the next one."

"No. Once you do a full workout at this range without it exhausting you so much, we go up. Maybe in a few days. You do it gradual."

But in two days, she'd be gone. Unless she decided to stay.

His tone changed. ""Believe me, I'm just as eager for you to get back into shape. I don't want anyone making fun of your ass. I'd have to beat them up, even though I kind of agree that your ass is a little spongy right now."

Picking up the two-pound girly weight she was sure he'd dug up for her, unless he did finger or toe lifts, she hurled it in the direction of his voice. At his satisfying grunt, she put her hands on her hips. "You don't know what a fine ass is, white boy."

"Oh, yeah? I know an attack on a superior officer when I feel it."

She recognized the mock threat in his voice, and was off the bench, backing up into a more open space. He'd given her the room's layout and, unlike the apartment, she could recall everything. Her hand followed the wall as she anticipated his approach, though of course she couldn't hear his steps unless he approached like a clog dancer.

It didn't matter. Launching the sparring match with a frontal attack, he kept her moving, back and forth across the mats. He called out his moves beforehand, letting her know when they were approaching the boundaries of the room, but like everything else, he pushed her a little past where she thought she could go. Whiny, pathetic Dana might have wanted to drop to the mat and surrender. But a stronger, earlier Dana surfaced, remembering her training, refusing to get cowed when she lost her balance from her hearing or sight loss handicap. Every time she did, he was there, catching her, bringing her back to her feet, keeping her going until she was winded again.

And feeling better, despite it all.

～

An hour later, they sat side by side on the screened porch, eating breakfast. Well, he sat, while she wilted into a chair like a limp rag. She had managed to help him in the kitchen, bringing him things and getting familiar with the layout there. Despite her weariness, she was ravenous, probably for the first time in months.

"You a good cook?"

She stopped in mid-bite. "Yes. Well, I was."

"What, you don't think you are anymore? Did you lose your memory?"

"Yes, I can cook," she grated, tearing the toast in half and finding the jelly.

"Make me one of those as well." He put his slice of toast next to her hand, guiding her fingers to it. "I like it pretty thick."

"Why do you want to know if I can cook?"

"Well, if you only want to sit in a house for the rest of your life, I figured you could cook and clean for me, be my sex slave. It'll be a win-win."

She bared her teeth in his direction. "Fuck off, Captain."

"Feisty. Your mouth gets you in trouble a lot, Sergeant." He touched her lips, though, brushed her cheek with his knuckles in a tender gesture that made her want to dip her head into his hand again. Feel his pulse and strength through his fingers, the warmth and support. Instead she cleared her throat and returned to her breakfast.

"So, I'm doing better this morning. Maybe we shouldn't go out tonight, you know. No need to rush things."

As the silence drew out, she cursed her mistake, even as her toes curled at the pause. She swallowed, something new rising up in her. "I'm sorry, Master. I'm trying to control things again."

"Yes, you are. Let it happen again and you'll finish up your workout with your glutes smarting from something other than squats."

He'd said it wasn't her job to worry. She was supposed to follow orders. He was right. She'd gone, eyes wide-open, into a firefight. Why going into a BDSM club could so terrify her, she didn't know, but it had been this way since her injury. Without her eyes, her hearing so diminished, things frightened her so much more easily. But in a short time, he'd shown her there were things she could detect that others couldn't, and those senses could help her. But she still feared the helplessness, the possible abyss that could yawn before her, swallowing her before she knew it was there.

She put down her sandwich, reached out. He was sitting next to her, and yet it was still a gratifying surprise to feel his hand close over hers instantly. "I'm scared, Master. Really, really scared."

It was hard to admit, even without seeing his face. The words nearly strangled her. But then his arms were around her, sliding her onto his lap so he could rock her.

"I know. I wish I could take away your fear, but the only way I know to do it is to help you face it. I'd face it for you if I could."

The truth of it was in the fierceness in his voice, a depth of feeling she wasn't sure she could handle, let alone believe. He tightened his grip on her. "It takes years for a Master to earn the trust I'm asking for from you. But I know how tough you are, deep inside. I know you want to trust me. I'm not going to do anything to let you down, all right?" He pressed a kiss to her temple; then she felt his lips curve. "What if I promise to keep your mind and luscious body so occupied with terribly sinful thoughts, fear won't have a chance of sliding into your mind?"

She wasn't sure anything could eliminate all worry from her mind, but she was more than willing for him to try. When she managed another nod, he slid his hands down her back, squeezed a buttock. "Finish your breakfast. Time to take you on a boat ride."

Peter knew she was afraid. He ached to tell her that she didn't have to do anything, that he'd protect her from everything. Every instance of pain or fear she had tore him apart inside. She'd had months, but it was still new to him. He wanted to grieve with her for what she'd lost, let her know the utter terror he'd felt at the idea of her being gone from his life before she'd really fully entered it.

Instead, he went back into the bedroom, took a few steadying breaths, and then brought her jeans to her, along with a long-sleeved knit cotton top borrowed from Cass's younger sister, who was a similar size to Dana. Next he applied bug spray, a necessary preparation for poling through the bayou abutting his property. The lemon insecticide had a smell strong enough to make her nose wrinkle, but helping her smooth it into her forearms, the slim neck and her ankles above the socks of her small sneakers, made him want to touch her more.

Though he'd found an avenue through her wary shields through Dominance and submission, he wasn't playing kung fu Master to her Grasshopper. He wanted to fuck her senseless, detonate an emotional and physical explosion that would deplete both of them. He wasn't a saint, for Christ's sake.

Getting outside on the boat dock and into the boat helped settle him, though things far deeper than his cock were stirred by their drifting progress as they poled away from the pilings. She hadn't felt comfortable sitting on the opposite bench, so he eased her to her knees in the bottom of the wooden craft, between his feet. As he moved through the marshland he loved, she pillowed her head on his knee, her hands loosely wrapped around his calf. Dana noted the myriad bird and insect life, asked him to identify the calls and warbles that were loud enough for her to hear. He told her about the others, tried to imitate them and almost coaxed a laugh out of her.

She registered humidity and temperature, depending on whether they were moving through quiet shadows or bright, lazy sun patches. Though she'd sneered at the compensatory benefit of her heightened senses, she unconsciously reached for those abilities. As they passed under the branches hanging over the water, she felt the lace of Spanish moss teasing their shoulders. When she trailed her fingers in the water, he watched the flow through the slim digits, the pull of cotton across her breasts as she twisted. He'd refused to let her wear a bra, wanting the pleasure of her nipples. The temptation of those peaks made him want to press her back on the bench, lift the shirt and suckle her, let her sigh and squirm as the boat drifted.

But her head was back on his knee, her fingers idly playing with the seam of his jeans' leg. She was getting sleepy, and that was okay. He wanted every day to be like this. He wanted to go to work, knowing she was going to be part of his life at the end of the day, on the weekends. Maybe she'd call him at lunch, from whatever job she'd be doing. He knew she was too damn smart to settle for sitting in a chair listening to the piercing shrieks of swamp birds, though there were few things more pleasurable to do on a lazy afternoon than that.

He wanted her to have her own life. Even so, a part of him liked the image he'd painted earlier, a 24/7 sex slave. It appealed to his protective side. Of course, a smart Master knew that a fully Dominant nature had to be reined in, the same way a submissive couldn't allow her own cravings to overwhelm her self-determination. Right now, he had to hold on to that balance for both of them. When she got her feet back under her, she could help him keep his urges in check, with that smart mouth he knew she had.

The thought warmed him, made him smile. Tenderness swamped him as he saw she'd fallen asleep. He held her cradled between his knees, moving slow and steady through the waters she'd feared earlier. One step at a time, one fear at a time.

Despite her murmured protest that she could walk, when he tied them off at the dock, he carried her up the boardwalk, into the house and to their bedroom, laying her on the covers. "I'll go run you a bath while you wake up a bit."

"My own personal servant," she said groggily, but there was an impudent quirk to her lips. "Isn't it supposed to be the other way around?"

"When a Master demands it, a slave serves, and serves him well. But a Master takes good care of his slave. That's the way it works."

Her lips pressed together. While her green gaze was sadly vacant, a yearning expression filled it abruptly. "We want you, Master," she said in a throaty voice. "Please. Soft and quiet, here on the bed. Let me know you're here, a part of me."

That expression reflected a desperate desire to believe in what he was offering, spoken and unspoken. It was also a painful reminder that, as much as he wanted to do so, he couldn't heal everything within her in a couple days. Even the goals he'd set, to pull her back from the desolate edge of darkness and help her find the courage to stay with him, might be more than could be accomplished in the time he had.

No. If that was all the time he had, he *would* make it work.

He could tease her, play with her, drive her to screaming climax, but in the face of that appeal for lovemaking, he was the one at her mercy. Unfastening her jeans, he took them off her legs, along with socks and shoes. He kept the tee on, liking the way her nipples pushed against the fabric, the points sharp in their arousal. If she curled her arms around him, would he lose all control? Bury himself in her, surround her and never let her be a foot away from him?

"I'm not sure this is the right time for this," he said quietly.

"No one's touched me for so long, Peter. Not like this. Like I'm real and..."

"Not broken?"

Reaching up, she touched his face. "Yeah. But I am broken, aren't I?"

She was killing him. He circled her wrist, held it and turned his mouth into her palm, nuzzling. "You're wounded, sweetheart. That's all. You'll heal, if you give yourself a chance."

Her fingers curled into his shirt, nails biting in. "I need you so badly right now. All the way into my heart."

"I want to give you that. But... I don't want to piss you off, but I really don't think you're ready. I also think it'll be better for you tonight, if we hold off, build it up in you." In the face of her whispered plea, the emotions she was tearing loose in his chest, he couldn't hold on to the stern Master he knew he should be. Blowing out a breath, he drew her hand down so she could feel she wasn't alone in her desire. "Hell, this is a bitch for me, too."

Dana swallowed at the size of him. "Do you have to be so damned honorable?"

"Believe me, honorable is not the deal here." He molded her fingers over him, held her grip there tight. "I don't want to win the battle, Dana. I want to take the field, win the war. When I make love to you in this bed, it's going to be because you've accepted you're with the man and the Master you want for the rest of your life."

"Peter, there's no way... We barely know each other."

"That ground's already been covered. Come on. Let's get that bug spray off of you and start getting you pampered and prepped for later tonight."

"You promised that you'd give me something to make me not afraid."

"I will. After a bath. Now, stop being all puppyish or I'll give you a spanking for turning your Master into a big softy."

He wondered if she realized how close he was to his own edge, particularly as he watched her struggle to rein it back in. Then her chin lifted. "I bet you cry at Hallmark movies."

"To even suggest I watch Hallmark movies is pushing past the line, little girl." Lifting her and taking a quick nip at her quivering mouth, he took her to the tub. As he ran the water, he removed her T-shirt, grazing his knuckles over the taut peaks.

"You do like tits, don't you?" she gasped.

"More than God and country," he said gravely. "And yours are gorgeous." He guided her in, helped her sit and adjusted the temperature. "Open your legs."

Surprise crossed her face, but she complied. Removing the small waterproof dual-headed vibrator from a drawer, he caressed her inner thighs with it, letting her get a sense of what he was doing before easing it into her pussy and her rectum. She had gorgeous legs and, though they were out of shape now, the skin was still silky, giving. He couldn't help thinking of how they'd feel wrapped around his back. He teased dark curls before he positioned the device and she bit her lip, her nipples jutting further.

It had no more than an inch of penetration, slim straps anchoring it in place and allowing him to position the clit teaser. She did that little breath-caught-in-the-throat thing while he made the adjustment, but when he turned it on a low level, her response was gratifying. She arched up, water sloshing against the sides, her nipples hardening further, challenging him to prove the truth of his convictions. Sliding his hand beneath her back, he brought his mouth to the closest one, taking it in like a small, swollen grape, suckling it so that she pushed her feet against the end of the tub, moving rhythmically against the vibrator. He laid his hands on her hips, stilling her.

"Enough of that. You stay still, move only as I need you to move.

Your pretty pussy is going to weep and ache for my cock and the release I'll grant it later tonight. This is all about preparing you to serve me tonight, any way I demand. I know you haven't forgotten how to serve a Master."

Her pulse elevated in her throat, her fingers curling under the water against her trembling thighs. God, she was going to kill him. She responded to his every order. Whether with sass and fire or soft entreaties, or tentative trust, she responded. And whether or not she realized it, by responding as a submissive, she was responding as the unwounded spirit he knew still lay within her.

It was a cynical world, one that had long ago abandoned love-at-first-sight to the very young and foolish. But his gut didn't lie to him, and her response to him told him he was right. It connected to things down deep in both their souls; he was sure of it. If she'd come back whole, he would have pursued her surrender as fiercely as he was doing now. Could he convince her of that, in less than forty-eight hours?

~

By the time he let Dana out of the tub, she was very clean and completely mindless. Since she had to clutch his shirt for balance as he walked her backward into the bedroom, she eagerly traced the way his waist muscles shifted with the movement, his abdominals tense with self-restraint.

When he left her standing in the middle of the room, he squeezed her hands, held on to them to the full reach of their arms before regretfully letting her go. It might be how aroused she was, but as she listened to him rustle in the closet, Dana actually felt as if he might be seeing a beautiful submissive standing in the center of his bedroom, her ass cocked in a provocative manner, the slim line of spine and nape so tempting, particularly with his collar still on her throat. He hadn't yet taken it off, and she didn't want him to do so.

She still wore his toy, though he'd added a harness to hold it in place. The dual vibrator changed speeds and sensations frequently, keeping her at a high peak. If his intent was to prepare her for tonight, she was ready. Hell, at this point, she might do a whole football team, if it meant Peter's cock would slide into her at the end, bringing her home inside herself.

The unexpected thought brought a lurch of emotion.

"Come stand over here, by the bed." When he got her there, he sat down on it, trapping her between his knees, settling his hands on her hips. That mere touch made her moan, thrust toward him shamelessly. He kneaded her buttocks, soothing and stirring at once. "That's it, baby. You're so hot for me now, aren't you?" Spreading his fingers, he tapped on the anal plug, making her grab hold of him for balance. "Tonight there are a couple things I want you to do for me. One, accept that you're beautiful. No hunching over, hiding yourself. Second, remember that you can trust me completely. I promise I'll keep you safe. There will be nothing for you to fear. All right?"

Though she jerked her head in a nod, she couldn't help the frisson of worry that shivered across her skin. His hands tightened on her. "I know it's going to be difficult. Which is why I think an additional training aid is necessary to focus your mind where it should be."

His hands left her as he picked something up. "We talked about this, that first night. I'm going to wrap you in a physical reminder of your Master's protection, my demand for your obedience to my will."

The stiff satin caressed her flesh, laces feathering across her skin.

A corset.

...keeping her straight and proud, knowing she's got nothing to worry about. Because she's mine.

"You liked that idea, wanted it bad. I could tell, enough that I wished I'd had one around that night. I even started a letter that would give you a play-by-play of how I'd lace you into one, but two paragraphs in, I was so hard I knew I couldn't finish it without embarrassing myself. This one isn't as custom fitted as I like, but we'll get you one that is soon. Lift your arms over your head."

Dana didn't think she could get more aroused, but the constriction of a corset made the impossible possible. As he wrapped it around her and began hooking it down the front, his knuckles teased her breasts. Clear desire trickled over her thighs, earning an approving growl from him. He took his time, as he had earlier with the fondling and suckling of her breasts, working his way down, finishing mere inches above her pubic bone. Then he turned her and went to work on the laces.

He told her the strapless corset was a copper color. As he tightened the laces, her breasts were bound and displayed at once, in that high pillow-top way that men found irresistible. Risking punishment, she lowered one hand to feel it, and suppressed a smile when he grunted a rebuke, one with a growl of lust in it. She raised the hand again. She couldn't stop herself from responding to his every touch. Her enhanced sense of taste and smell made it worse. If he grazed her breast, she arched. If he slid a palm over her buttock, she pushed back into his hand, wishing she could grind down on him. Every lacing made her feel more restrained, and *his*, at once, and damned if he wasn't right. Being encased in it lifted her body, straightened her spine, made her feel as if she could do anything. Including be beautiful. Her Master would cherish her, keep her from harm.

A long time ago, she'd wished for one night of a fairy tale. She'd gotten her desire, but she wondered if tonight would truly be the answer to her dreams, in the gods sometimes tragic way of granting wishes. It didn't matter; she'd take it.

Let me be lost in this, if only for tonight. Forget everything else and believe I can see. She could already imagine how he looked in every detail. Somehow she knew his every expression, though she hadn't had the opportunity to see many. Maybe it was because she'd fantasized so much about him, all those many months. But she wanted the opportunity to put her fingers on his face, actually feel what his facial muscles did as he smiled, laughed, frowned, concentrated...came.

She mewled as he removed the vibrator and harness, caressing her before setting them aside. "You're so fucking hot and sexy. I wish you could see yourself. Every man there's going to wish you were his to fuck."

The unadorned male evaluation, spoken straight from his cock, was more believable than a hundred praises calculated to charm. When nylon rope stroked against her cheek, he let her touch it, follow it to the end to find the metal fastener. Without a command, she dropped her head back so he could attach the tether to the ring on the collar, above the St. Christopher's pendant.

He placed his lips there first, the sensitized skin above the collar, and she cried out, but kept her hands above her head as he'd ordered.

When he drew back, he made an approving noise. "This is yours. When we get there, you'll wear this at all times. You'll feel my touch through it. It's ten feet long. Inside any range I pay out, you can touch and explore without fear."

When his fingers collared her even above the strap, she dipped her head, touched the tip of her tongue to his knuckle. "I intend to show you off, and take fierce pleasure in knowing you're mine. Mine to fuck in front of them if I want, or have you suck me off at a table while I share a drink with my friends. Sit you on my lap and let you go to sleep when you get tired. Dwell on the pleasure of having you in my bed."

She'd never had a Master she trusted enough to go quite that public. So the searing pleasure of the idea with Peter surprised her. Belonging to him, serving him in front of others. She would feel their eyes upon her, the heat of their lust pressing on her as she served her Master.

As if he could follow her thoughts—and maybe he could, because she was sure her face reflected her arousal—he spoke in a voice laden with demanding lust. "Practice being on this leash. Give me the lap dance of my life, as if I'd ordered you to do it there. Grind yourself down on me the way I know you want to, showing those other guys what they're missing. And always remember—you belong to me."

She'd been a good dancer, but that had been then. Self-consciousness arose, but at an encouraging murmur, she grasped for confidence. It didn't hurt that he had her so jacked up from his touch and that vibrator, she was a creature of pure sex right now.

He must have had a remote on the bed, because though he hadn't moved, the reverberation of a bass line came through her soles seconds before the music reached her ears, drowning out everything but what he wanted her to do. It was a hard rock piece with lots of drums, a blatant pounding sex rhythm. Letting the music penetrate, she swayed, shifting from one hip to the other, getting the sense of it. She visualized nightclubs where she'd worn silky, scanty dresses, danced with friends, or found a good-looking boy and enjoyed, rubbing herself against him in some outrageous dance moves.

But even then she hadn't wanted just hot, sweaty sex. She wanted the guy who would tolerate only so much teasing, the flashes of ass and leg goading him to take her over, take her in hand, make her feel the invisible bonds he had on her at all times, with or without a collar.

Of course, if that boy had been Peter, she'd let the strap of her dress drop off her shoulder, the neckline of the dress getting dangerously low, drawing his eye to the wobble of the breasts in danger of full exposure.

Now, though, she didn't have to imagine such a thing. She wore his corset, binding her from breast to low on her hips, making her hyperaware of her exposed cleavage, the curve of her buttocks. All on display for him.

She let desire flow through her like water, guiding her body into the first steps. As she rocked into it, she backed up, putting her hand on the leash. When it slid through her fingers, she registered how it became taut as she reached its length. She liked the idea of using the leash, knowing the man on the other end of it was holding on to the control, his attention on her drawn tight as that strap.

Turning, she wrapped herself in it, let it bind her arms and upper torso, augment the corset's constriction. When she reached him, her hands were trapped at her sides. One restrained hand found his spread knees and she turned, slid her backside low, down his abdomen, then lower. She put her ass in his lap and executed a rotation that gave her a mouthwatering idea of how hard his cock was.

Straddling his thigh, she teased her wet pussy along the line of the denim, then turned in a relatively lithe move she might not have been able to pull off before the morning's workout. Or tomorrow, when every muscle would be sore. Now she brought her thigh up against his testicles, shimmying down and up against them, imagining his eyes on her breasts, nearly in his face. She could feel his hot breath on them. Then she turned again, dancing back from him, unwrapping herself, only to follow the leash back in, her slim fingers teasing along it until she found him again.

She liked how the corset restricted her breathing, all of it a reminder she had nothing to fear, that he had her heart and soul encased in that satin cage. She sat herself down in his lap again, and this time used her hands braced on his knees to grind and bump herself against him.

"There's a mirror in front of you. I'm getting the best fucking view of your tits in that corset, the way you're bent over like that. Keep working your ass against my cock. I'm going to explode." A stinging slap on her thigh resulted in a pleasurable spasm in her pussy. "Not too much of the same rhythm, now. You keep your mind on pleasing me and not getting yourself off. That's for later."

Easier said than done. Damn, he was too intuitive. She varied the rhythm, but kept on with the dancing, switched back to a front straddle and rocked herself in front of his face. Holding on to his shoulders, she got her knees up onto the bed, her back immediately supported by his hands as she leaned back into his strength and figure-eighted her way across his cock. She had to be dampening his jeans, because she was soaked again.

Before her accident, she would have had the stomach muscles to hold the position for a longer time. Now, though, her muscles burning, she had to back off, but he slid her down and around, to cradle her in his lap. Closing his hand on the strap, he tugged on it near the D-ring, his fingers playing in her deep cleavage.

"Whose sweet slave are you?"

"Yours, Master," she said hoarsely. God, she remembered how she'd wondered if she'd ever find this, the one who could chain her, yet make her feel like her wings could stretch farther than she'd ever thought possible. Was it still possible to fly if you had to see yourself another way, through another's eyes?

Lust suddenly torn between something more serious, she touched his face, the slope of tough jaw. Felt him still as he picked up on her mood. "If I'd known it was going to be the last time I was going to see you..."

"It wasn't." Cupping her hands, he pressed them harder to him. "If you let me into your soul, let yourself be inside mine, you'll always see me more clearly than anyone."

"How do you know that?"

He brought his mouth close, touched hers. "You were miles and miles away for over a year, but I saw you every day, sweetheart. Every fucking day."

CHAPTER TEN

They were meeting at Lucas and Cassandra Adler's home, and taking a limo from there to the club. Peter had helped her don a wrap-around short black dress that was open in the front to show the corset's tenuous grasp on her breasts, and stockings with slim garters. He'd also left the collar on. She was a little discomfited, but he told her she looked like a sexy woman with a penchant for Goth jewelry. From his possessive, lingering touch on her thighs as he helped her don the stockings, she realized he'd integrated them for her confidence, not because he felt any part of her needed conceal-ment. All she felt were his desire and pleasure in touching her flesh.

As he handed her into his car and made sure her seat belt was secure, then dropped a kiss on the top of one breast, she drew in a shaky breath. The butterflies in her stomach were throwing rock grenades. She inhaled Peter's aftershave as he got in, a big man getting behind the wheel, making the car rock. He'd already turned on the seat heater for her, and she was grateful for the warmth coming through the upholstery, since the evening air had a nip.

"What kind of car is this?"

"You after my money now? Gold digger."

"Gram always said a good man with money was as easy to love as a good man with none." She sniffed. "But I'm only after your body, Captain."

"Well, then." He covered her cold hand with his, squeezed. As he rubbed a soothing thumb over her knuckles, he leaned over, brushed a kiss along the back of her ear, nuzzling there. Sliding his fingers into the seam of her thighs, he pressed until she parted them. "Leave them like that," he whispered into the microphone of her hearing aid so she caught the sensual purr close up. "I want to play with your pussy while I drive. I'm going to keep you talking the whole way, so I can hear your voice break as I get you hotter and hotter."

As a distraction technique, it was unbeatable, tangling her nerves back up into full-blown lust until she could barely think. By the time they pulled into the Adlers' driveway, her breath was fast and shallow. The tiny thong was in danger of dripping, she was sure. But she heard a console opening, a moment before he pressed an absorbent cloth against her, making her start up against his hand and grind herself there like a wanton, her hand falling onto his forearm, gripping it for an anchor.

"I'm making you into a mindless little slut, aren't I?" He murmured it against her ear again, his body close and hard next to her. Lunging, she met his lips in hot, openmouthed need, and thank God, he didn't deny her. He captured her movement, controlling it with a hand to her nape. Sucking on her tongue, he thrust his in with a demand that incinerated even hers. When his hand sealed over her pussy, not to stroke but to grip, a reminder of his possession, she moaned against his lips.

"Remember," he growled as he broke free at last, "that you're *my* mindless little slut."

"Yes, Master," she breathed, even as she trembled. Her fantasies hadn't done justice to a Master this dominant, one so overwhelming. The healthy, whole Dana would have loved it, but this Dana wondered if it would be too easy to give in to it, damn him to a life of watching after her physical shortcomings. In truth he seemed completely comfortable—or totally oblivious—to such shortcomings. That might be dangerous, too, because his confidence might make her crazy enough to start believing this was possible.

Peter Winston was as sure as hell of himself, which made her hope all the more painful. Two days didn't a new life make. It was only the start, and maybe he really didn't realize everything that was involved. If she agreed to stay longer, could she handle the agony if he changed his mind? How long would it take before she was strong enough to handle a setback like that? And if he realized it was a mistake, and tried to stay with her out of pity, she'd just die. It was easy to say she wasn't a coward; far harder to prove it to herself.

He was taking her around the back, through a pool area. Though she smelled the chlorine, he described the area to her in precise military detail. His friends were at a tiki bar about forty feet away, mixing drinks. Vaguely, she picked up greetings, and clearly heard Peter's response. As he guided her along the concrete, he had a hand at the small of her back, one of her hands in his. Despite that, she tucked her other hand back to touch his fingertips on her hip, trying not to cling or show fear of tripping.

Then another, uncomfortably familiar scent came to her nostrils. Her steps slowed and she cocked her head. "Is there someone to our left?"

"Yes. Cassandra's brother, Jeremy. He's sitting in one of the pool loungers, about ten feet from you. I was going to introduce you to him, but he appears to be dozing." The cautionary note in Peter's voice needed no translation. She'd been in a hospital long enough to recognize the stench of medical treatments, IVs, and sickly sweat. A combination impossible to erase, no matter how often the nurse bathed her.

"I'm awake." She heard a sluggish voice, raised to catch his attention and therefore reaching her ears. Then a murmur of sound that Peter translated.

"Jeremy said it's nice to meet you, Dana."

God, she hated that, when someone had to repeat something to her. But she supposed it wasn't the end of the world. Following an impulse, she moved toward the lounger, taking Peter with her by holding on to his hands. He stopped her, guided her around something in her way. Another lounger, according to what brushed her thigh.

Leaning down as the scent grew stronger, she found a thin leg, a drape of cloth that might be a robe. "I'm fine, Jeremy," she said. "It's nice to meet you." *See, Gram, I remembered my manners, even while being led around like a cart horse.*

"You might not want to touch me." Jeremy cleared his throat, spoke a little more loudly. "AIDS leper here. In fact, I could kick off at any time. Sis has to check with a mirror to see if I'm breathing, or if it's time to take out the garbage."

Peter winced at Jeremy's usual caustic take on things. Though he could tell Dana had heard him clearly, her hand had not moved from its position on his leg. Cassandra was walking toward them. From her expression of quiet pain, he knew she'd heard her brother's comment, though he was sure she'd heard his cynical humor before.

Lucas came with her, sliding a hand around her waist. He shot Jeremy a guys-giving-each-other-shit look. Peter thanked God for his sensitive friends when Lucas took his voice up several octaves. "Yeah, knowing his inconsiderate ass, he'll stay alive a day after the usual trash pickup, so we have to put him on ice for a week."

Dana sank down on the edge of the lounger, found Jeremy's sleeve, followed it to his hand, and slid her fingers in between his. "Your voice," she mused. "It sounds a bit like my brother's. You're too young."

"You're too pretty to be a jarhead."

"That's a Marine term," she said primly. "But thanks."

As Peter watched her, the way her hand moved carefully over Jeremy's thin fingers, he suspected his curiosity mirrored Jeremy's. The young man stared at their hands.

"You must really like your brother. You're touching me, and you don't even know me."

"He died some time ago. That's why I needed to touch you." A faint smile crossed her face, but there was no humor in it. "Sometimes when you can't see, you have to touch to be sure. I hear his voice sometimes. I heard his voice for a while. " Her voice drifted off and Peter saw the moisture gather in her eyes, but even as he stepped closer, she shook it off, gave Jeremy an arch look, despite her inability to look directly at him. "You think after being blown up, I'm really worried about you sneezing on me? If someone wanted to kill me, they've already tried hard enough. I could show you some scary scars."

"Though I much rather you didn't," Peter put in, instigating a competitive spark in Jeremy's face, cynicism briefly replaced by wry humor.

"Hey, she may find the emaciated look sexy, versus your beefcake routine."

"No doubt," Peter said dryly.

Aside from Jeremy's sickly aroma, the subtle sadness in Peter's tone told Dana the boy looked bad. It was amazing how much she could pick up from voices, even when she couldn't always hear the words clearly. Ironically, her comprehension improved when she stopped worrying about hearing the response, instead focusing on the emotions she was hearing. Jeremy was frightened. Perhaps that was why, though he was obviously close to slipping into sleep again, he'd wanted to be out here, around people, voices and light, because darkness was closing in.

She'd had the opposite reaction, wanting to withdraw when she knew the loss of light would be a permanent fact of her life, not a transition to death. Gram had always said, "People ain't happy with nothing. God blesses them, they complain. Bad things happen, they complain. They can't think about nothing but themselves, though the whole world's full of people worse off they could be helping to feel better."

Following impulse, she found Jeremy's face with her fingertips, leaned in to press her lips against the gaunt cheek, holding herself there. His hand came up, gripped her arm. Long, skinny fingers. Cold. The boy was so cold. He needed another blanket.

"There's nothing to fear," she whispered. "All you're doing is stepping into God's arms." Gram had said that, too, when her brothers were killed. *Stepping into God's arms.*

"I'm not all that religious," he said, voice breaking.

She'd found the right crevice. People were all cracks and crevices. Since people got more of those as they lived and lost, it was sometimes hard to find the right opening to a young heart. But for this boy, it was one large Grand Canyon, easy for someone—she swallowed— easy for someone with the eyes to see it.

I wanted to be a minister...

"My Gram said religion only matters to men, not to God. Your heart belongs to Him, and He's always there to welcome it back, like a mama's arms. Or a sister's," she added, remembering what Peter had told her in the car. Cassandra had raised her siblings.

Jeremy's breath was a little uneven, his hands gripping her arms hard, a wordless thanks. As she eased him back, stroked his brow, she could tell even that little exertion had depleted him. He relaxed, sleeping again. When Peter's hand covered hers, she let him lift her to her feet, guide her away from the lounge chair. His fingers grazed her cheek. "There you are," he murmured. "The girl I met in that club. As far as *my* heart goes, you have it, sweetheart. God's going to have to fight you for it."

"Not the only one." A deep timbre reached out to her along with another male hand, giving hers a squeeze. "Lucas Adler. I'm pleased to meet you, Dana."

"I'm Cassandra."

Before Dana expected it, she was eased into a friendly female hug, one with some heavy emotion behind it. Long hair brushed her cheek, smooth skin against the faint texture of her healing scars. "Thank you for what you just did. Because of Peter, you were already welcome here, but consider yourself welcome anytime."

"Even without his deadbeat ass," another voice put in, and her hand was taken in a new strong grasp. "I'm Ben."

She didn't need eyes to know the two men were tall, a little dangerous and a lot sexy. With the sensory overload Peter had inflicted on her up to now, her body fairly vibrated in response to any stimulus. It hadn't occurred to her eye candy would still have an effect on her, but apparently it was misnamed. A good-looking man had a way of appealing to more than one sense. Peter had already proven that to her. She cleared her throat, tried to rally the spirit belonging to that girl Peter remembered.

"You must be the slick lawyer."

"I see he's already set you against me. He's insecure that way. Afraid I'll take you right out from under his nose."

O'Neill crossed her mind. His teasing, the playful sexual innuendos. He'd come to see her when they'd both been at Walter Reed. She gave him kudos for coming more than once, because she'd been a bitch most of the time. She should have been kinder, more responsive, because in hindsight, she realized he suffered guilt over her injuries. He'd healed, with only a harrowing scar to impress the girls, but psychological wounds could fester. Maybe she'd write or e-mail him. Peter would help her.

Now, though, she tuned back in to her immediate surroundings, lifting a brow in Ben's direction. "Men tend to underestimate a short woman's ability to kick their balls into the back of their throat. Lower center of gravity and all."

"Ouch," Ben responded, a grin in his voice. "Peter, I'm definitely going to take my shot."

"I'm sure," her escort said. Peter's touch slid down her back, giving her buttock a caress. The pressure of his hand against the stiff corset, giving way to the thin fabric and her accessible flesh beneath it, riveted all her nerve endings toward that point. The caress made her already aroused body even more so, such that she was glad another introduction was forthcoming, letting her catch her breath.

"I'm Matt Kensington, Dana. It's a pleasure to have you join us. This is my wife, Savannah."

There was a charisma to that voice, a rolling power to the grip that confirmed he was the leader of this pack, because the position of Peter's body changed, a shift as if he was presenting her for approval. Then she felt Savannah's cool, slim fingers, a welcoming, firm hold. Aside from that, the brace of diamonds on her wedding ring was enough to tempt a closer investigation, because Peter was right. Dana *did* like jewelry.

"Thank you for what you did in Iraq," Savannah said quietly. "Your sacrifice means so much to us all. If you need anything, you need only ask."

She wasn't sure what to do with that, but then she met the last member of Peter's unusual circle of close friends.

"Jon." This voice was tranquil, a sexy almost-like-a-dream quality to it. "Dana, when you're comfortable, I've been studying some impressive advances in sensory technology that may interest you."

"Jon's our mechanical genius." Peter's caress again. "In a variety of ways. The device you experienced earlier today is one of his far simpler ones."

Dana cleared her throat, glad for once she couldn't see because she was sure she'd blush up to her roots meeting Jon's knowing gaze. "It was...effective."

"Glad you enjoyed it." Jon's sensitive, clever fingers enclosed hers, stroking her palm, an easy intimacy that seemed to reflect the way they'd all touched her. As if somehow by being Peter's, she was part of an inner circle, provocative and calming at once.

In the car, Peter had reminded her all four men were sexual Dominants, their attitudes and preferences like his own. She hadn't really believed it, but now, in their presence, there was no doubt. In another situation fear might have trickled through her, wondering how much she really knew about Peter, taking her to a BDSM club with his friends. But, despite the different quality and mannerisms to each, they had that same humming undercurrent that Peter had.

Firm, confident sexuality with an underlying...tenderness. Protective. It acknowledged the fears she might be facing, and yet sent them a message: *Nothing's going to happen to you while we have anything to say about it.*

On top of that, in Cass's and Savannah's voices, she heard the purring ease that reflected well-loved women. And finally, even if she was putting too much stock in this test flight of her other senses, it didn't change one inexplicable fact—she trusted Peter.

He'd plunged right into her shit without any invitation. He'd been overbearing and pushy, a bully in every sensual, protective way. There wasn't anything cruel about him. He might frustrate the hell out of her, such that, if she had any intention of accepting his ludicrous offer to stay, she'd occasionally have to hit him in the head with a blunt object while he slept. But he'd never let anything hurt her. Even if she was too uncertain of her handicap for her irrational mind to accept it, her rational mind did.

"Let's have a drink and get to know one another," Matt suggested, the masculine Texas drawl in his voice as alluring to a woman's senses as she suspected the rest of him was. "Then we'll go."

While Peter and Lucas lifted the sleeping Jeremy and carried him back to his room, where his younger sister Marcie would tend him that evening, Cass and Savannah guided Dana to a circular sofa arrangement. Used to being self-conscious, worried about what sentences she might miss, she found it amazing that this group of strangers so quickly dispelled her anxiety, on those issues at least.

Dana felt no catty or pitying vibes from Cassandra and Savannah at all. They integrated her into the conversation, drawing out information on her interests and pointing her toward shopping and recreational activities in the area they'd love to visit with her. She hadn't felt so easily accepted since basic training.

When Peter returned and settled next to her, the group dove into cocktails, catching up on business, some social talk. As the men moved around, it brought her the distracting, pleasurable scents of male heat, cologne, aftershave, dry-cleaned silk and cotton.

The first one to touch her was Jon. A casual brush of her knee accompanied the courteous, "Would you like another drink, Dana?"

As Ben and Lucas stood behind the couch, exchanging opinions with Peter on some business matter, Lucas's thumb and forefinger circled her nape, a light pressure as he leaned over to respond to his wife's gentle reproof about talking business. Ben followed it up with a joke about being henpecked, and his knuckles slid along the point of Dana's shoulder.

Then, a few moments later, as Matt passed by, he made a brief stop, dropping to his heels she assumed to do what he did—grip her ankle in a large hand, his fingers caressing her as he straightened the strap of Dana's sandal for her. Then his touch slid away, leaving a definite impression on her highly sensitive nerve endings.

It was as if each of the men were taking turns with the sensual but respectful caresses. But it was when Matt Kensington did it she realized—with shock—their intent.

They were marking her. Identifying her as part of the pack, but also helping her to recognize them that way as well.

She could be crazy, but she was almost certain she wasn't. Instead, she was impressed by their intuitive understanding of how it reassured her, to have tactile imprints to anchor and center her.

Beyond that noble purpose, it enhanced the charge of sexual anticipation flavoring the air, since they all knew where they were going tonight. Peter had his arm stretched behind her, and she was hyperaware whenever he dropped his hand from the couch to tease her collarbone. Once, his other hand settled on her leg, gliding up her thigh. Just a brief, sweet caress to the inside. Before she thought, she'd started to spread her legs, a submissive's automatic response to a Master's touch there. He gripped her smoothly, stopping her, but before she could get discomfited, his lips brushed her ear in approval.

Cassandra and Savannah were both submissives, she reminded herself. Since she knew the nature of a submissive, she wasn't surprised they were successful businesswomen. The fact they gave their men a lot of playful shit was a bonus, one that had her laughing and joining in the banter herself. Peter threatened to take her home before they taught her bad habits.

Home. It didn't sound as odd as she would expect. She let that thought bolster her when they finally headed out to the club.

~

More conversation, the scent of champagne and truffles, and then a chocolate-covered strawberry Peter fed to her directly from his own mouth, settling his lips over hers as she laid back in the cradle of his arm in the spacious limo. The taste of the fruit and confection melted her body into the insistent strength of his.

"Hell," Ben groused from the seat across from them. "Way to get my dick hard before we get there, Peter. Ease up or I'm going to jump the first pretty ass I see."

"Like you need an excuse," Jon observed wryly. "When we went to St. Bart's, I thought they were going to kick us off the island."

As Peter lifted his head at last, Dana drew in a ragged breath. "Just how rich are you all?"

"Peter's a poor cousin, really." Ben's knee grazed hers, then his calf as he stretched out a long leg on the side opposite of Peter. "One of those hangers-on that sponges off his betters. We tolerate him because his whole soldier routine attracts women. You'd be much better off with a lawyer."

"Particularly a castrated one," Peter said.

"Peter is quite well-off, Dana," Savannah reassured her. "You don't have to worry about working two or three jobs to support him."

Dana let herself smile. "Well, as long as he's not after *my* fortune. I have two or three of these kind of limos lying around, you know."

Then her stomach was jumping again, because the limo pulled in the club parking lot. She tried to calm it, focusing on Peter's reassuring grip on her hand. While Surreal was not as upscale as The Zone, Peter had said it was still one of Louisiana's best clubs, doing its best to emulate The Zone's example on the more limited budget it had. As the others got out, she was hit by a wave of loud voices and white noise. Heat and a flicker at the corners of her dark vision suggested a lot of flashing light. "It's busy tonight," Jon mentioned, as he exited the limo last.

She hadn't moved, both hands clutched around Peter's one large one, resting in her lap. His fingers bracketed her thigh, squeezed. "You trust me, sweetheart?"

"I want to. I'm scared, though. And I hate it. I don't think I can do this. Please don't make me do this." Her breath was starting to come faster. Fuck being calm. That wasn't going to work. She'd been crazy to agree to this.

For months, being blind and mostly deaf had made her unsure of herself, frightened by new things in a way she'd never been. It was easier and safer to stay within her comfort zone, with people she knew, places that were familiar. People could call it a crutch, but they didn't fucking know what it was like. What had she been thinking? Her good sense had been fogged by sex—that was what it was. Hell, she'd hardly known she still had a libido until Peter came to find her. Okay, yeah, she'd fantasized about him all the time, but like a dream, not a reality. This was reality, big-time, up close and way too freaking personal.

"Hey, hey." He cupped her face. "Focus on me. Breathe. Breathe slow and deep. There is nothing to be scared of here. You remember why?"

She swallowed. "No, no, I don't. Peter, please—"

"Because I'm not going to let anything happen to you. Say it."

His fingers were stroking her face and she could feel how close he was. Hell, he'd pulled her into his lap, was cradling her, holding her... Well, she'd say like a child, except his fingers had slipped between her legs, and she was amazed as he used her earlier arousal to simply slide the tips of his fingers partway into her, past the thong. It centered everything there, throbbing, anxiety and lust tangled into a ball. "Say it, Dana."

"You're not going to let anything happen to me," she whispered, and gasped as his fingers twitched, sending pleasure spiraling hard and tight through her clit.

"Damn straight." Snapping on the leash, he gave her a tug, a sensual reminder of their afternoon. "Ten feet, remember?"

"It's a club, Peter. There will be people I don't know all around. " He'd said she should feel comfortable touching, but what about being touched? And strangers? His friends were okay; she'd met them, but—

"You've known you were a sub since you were a teen. Remember telling me that? Trust in that, Dana. Trust your Master."

When he brushed his lips over her temple, she pressed into that touch, squeezing her eyes shut. "I've got you." He said it against her ear, a habit she was beginning to like, particularly when he took a little nip at the earpiece of her hearing aid, an unexpected sexy caress. "Let's get you out of this."

Moving slow and easy, his fingers drifted down her sternum, molding over her left breast before he dipped down to the tie of the dress, loosened it and slid it off her shoulders. She'd be leaving it in the car, wearing only the corset, thong panties, stockings and low pair of heels he'd given her.

She'd worn as little the night she'd met him, less even, but she'd felt nowhere near as vulnerable as she did this night. Despite that, though, strangely, the removal of the outer garment almost seemed to help, because it truly left no doubt whose and what she was here. His slave. His submissive, under his guidance and protection.

"Here you go." When he bracketed her face, a mask slid down over it, one that fit her nose and around her eyes, but stopped there, leaving her mouth and chin free of encumbrance. Lifting her hands to it, she realized it was a remarkable likeness to the mask she'd worn for him that night.

"Now"—he found her right nipple beneath the corset, began to do a slow pinch and roll that made her mouth dry—"be whatever you want to be tonight, as long as you remember you're mine. This is your fairy tale, however you want it told. Anything that worries you, you tell me and I'll fix it. You hear?"

Tears threatened as she touched the mask, smoothed it under her fingers. "Peter, we can't live in a fairy tale."

Easing his touch up under her jaw, he cradled her face, and then she was close in his arms again. They wrapped around her back, her hands settling on his chest, curling into the cotton dress shirt he was wearing, the silk of his tie. "I'm giving you one tonight, Dana. I'm going to convince you that you *are* my happily ever after. I want to be yours, if you'll give me the chance."

She wasn't sure if he was teasing, and if she was crazy for wanting him not to be. So she summoned an indifferent smile, struggling for their earlier banter. "I don't know. I'll have to compare your portfolio to Ben's. You know I'm a gold digger."

"Hmm. Then let me give you something else to think about."

Catching her lips in an unexpectedly aggressive kiss, he put his hand back between her legs, massaging her clit, delving deep inside with devilishly clever and aggressive fingers that demanded nothing less than full surrender. The ambush caught her off guard. In less than five seconds, the climax took her like a fast rush of machine-gun fire, jerking her back against the cushions, her hands clutching at him for an anchor as he continued to kiss her senseless, her ass rubbing in frantic rhythm against him and the plush fabric of the seat.

He milked her to the end of it, took her down to a gasping, shuddering aftermath, and then nipped at her lips. "That's the last I want to hear about Ben's fucking portfolio."

"Sure," she said faintly. Though, privately, she thought if she ever wanted to be overwhelmed with a mindless climax within seconds, she'd shamelessly chant, "Ben, Ben, Ben," to elicit that reaction from her captain again.

She bit her lip, shuddering with an aftershock as he used a handkerchief to clean her, holding her thong to the side, rubbing her as she clutched his jacket sleeve. When he readjusted her clothes, she wondered if the handkerchief was his. If he left it on the seat with her scent, or put it back in his pocket to carry. Then he was getting out of the limo.

Her legs were trembling now for more reasons than nervousness, so he supported her as she emerged. She blessed him for thinking of the mask, which would conceal that her eyes were sightless. Taking a deep breath, she tried to imagine how she looked. The nightclub lights would gleam off the curves of breast, hip and waist encased in the copper corset, most of her scars beneath the garment and stockings. Her ass would be shown to good advantage in heels that were flattering but not ice pick or too high, Peter's sensitivity to her balance. She was going to have to look into that yoga instructor, and practicing walking. She did like how stilettos made her ass look. She thought Peter would, too, if she reacquired the confidence for that fuck-me-if-you-dare pendulum swing she'd had down pat before.

The clothes helped. Lord God, did they help, as every child who'd ever played dress up knew. Instead of being in a dark room in a sweat suit and mindless stupor, indifferent to her life, wallowed down in fearful misery, she stood in front of a BDSM club, in the company of a man who'd made it clear he thought her capable of anything. Who, despite what scars she might be showing, thought she was sexy, gorgeous. His.

It wasn't the clothes. It was him. The corset was his weapon, one he'd deployed with maximum devastating effect. With that Master's intuition he had, he'd discerned its power over her from nothing more than her brief reaction to the suggestion, on one far-too-short night, more than a year ago.

Before this had happened, she'd always believed in herself, her own strength. It shamed her, the way she'd faltered. In the army, she'd accepted certain things couldn't be accomplished alone. She just hadn't realized she might need someone to stand at her back even when it didn't involve AK-47s and insurgents.

Could she dare to hope he stood there for the right reasons, or was it pity? Powerful, deceptive nostalgia goaded by a titillating memory, instead of their present reality? She wondered if it was a sign her perspective was changing, that she was more worried about what was going on in his heart than her own. Was that good or bad?

His hand was on her hip, stroking the top of her buttock, his thigh pressed to the back of hers. Reaching down, she curled her fingers over his. They overlapped hers, his lips touching her throat below the collar, so that she tilted her head back to his shoulder, giving him immediate access.

"We're going inside now," he said. "It's going to be impossible to hear in certain places, okay? Pay attention to the leash, to my touch. If you get confused or disoriented, don't worry. I'm right here."

Leaning down, he brushed his cheek against hers once more. "We're going to have fun tonight. Right?" She latched on to the relaxed quality of his voice, tried to take it into herself, despite the fact she was all too aware that the human world was a very visual and auditory one, not one that encouraged touch. Even fetish clubs had stringent rules about touching anyone without invitation, though if there was a large segment that liked to play public, there were often a lot of invitations. But she couldn't see or hear any of those invitations.

Peter promised they would have fun, that he was here. She had to trust him to keep her out of trouble. Still, her pulse was pounding in her throat as he took her up the ramp toward the entrance, steadying her at the change in angle. He'd described it in detail on the way, so she focused on the image. Blue and silver lights outlining the main doorway, people in all manner of fetish garbs inside, paying their cover fee, having their IDs checked.

Peter and his friends were already members, so they passed through that area without much of a pause. It was crowded, though. Peter's hand was wrapped in the leash, lying on her hip, keeping her close, but she still bumped people. A brush of velvet from a cloak, smells of latex and leather, that humming vibration of arousal. Music from the approaching dance floor resonated through her feet. Realizing they must be passing through the public play area, she heard snatches of things. A muted, rhythmic sound she realized was a flogger. A cry of pain laced with pleasure, the plea to a Mistress for more.

Perhaps Peter would take her to a booth with his friends, get a drink. She could kneel at his feet. She wouldn't have to move, to fight the overwhelming urge to stretch out her arms and pinwheel, trying to figure out her surroundings.

When the crowd let up so she could breathe, move more freely, Peter eased away from her, letting the leash lengthen and slacken. Immediately she reached after him, but he was already beyond her fingertips. Before she could panic, the tether twitched. Not pulling her in that direction, merely letting her know he was there.

He was giving her ten feet to do as she pleased, but she didn't want to move. This spot was safe because she knew it. Ground solidly beneath her feet. It was way too soon. While the people were no longer crushed against her, there were still too many of them, stepping in and out of that personal space buffer. Too many scents, sounds, sensations, not the arousing mélange she'd experienced at the Adler home. It was too overwhelming.

Reaching up to grip the tether, she drew in the slack so she could determine and move in Peter's direction with slow, uncertain steps. She walked out of the shoes, needing to grip the floor with her toes, health laws be damned. Damn it, he kept moving, staying out of range. He wasn't going to let her cling to him. Frustration shot sparks through the anxiety. If she could see, this wouldn't scare her at all, not even if she was alone. But she wasn't alone. That light tug again. A reminder he was here. Nothing would harm her.

Then something unexpected happened. She had more space to breathe. Those strangers who'd been so close no longer were, though she still sensed a crush of people in the noise and air movement. Had they figured out she was handicapped in some way and moved back? Were they staring at her? No. She wore her mask and leash, so she was no more of a spectacle than any other submissive. Submissives were here to be seen, to serve.

Too many unknown variables. She struggled for calm, but even the reassurances weren't enough. *Oh, hell. I can't do this. I can't.* Here she was in the middle of vast amounts of people, a fish alone in an indifferent ocean carrying her where it would. Isolated, where sound was a distant cacophony she couldn't understand. How could he bring her here, when she'd been in virtual isolation for so long?

Why was he doing this to her? He should know better. She wasn't that same fucking Dana, was she?

"I can't do this," she said aloud, and then she shouted it, anxiety clawing raw at her throat. But her voice would simply be swallowed in all the other noise. That was the way the public areas could be. With a snarl, she wrapped her hands on the leash and jerked, a terrified, angry child wanting to bring him to her physically.

It came free in her hands, the strap slapping against her calves in gentle rhythm. Dana froze, her hands clutched on it. She'd pulled the leash from her Master's hands.

CHAPTER ELEVEN

*H*e couldn't be more than a few feet from her, right? A staccato of heartbeats later, however, she still didn't feel his reassuring touch, or a tug indicating the end of the leash had been picked up.

But then, he wouldn't, would he? He was there, but he was waiting on her. With Masters she'd had in the past, her interactions might have been fun, occasionally intense. That deep, soul-level bonding she'd sought with the right Master, who touched her submissive soul and achieved a link that went beyond posted rules, the one who understood it was a part of who she was and not just a way to liven up her sex life, had not appeared. Until Peter. He'd already proven he had a deeper understanding of her need to be Dominated than even she'd admitted. She trusted him on instinct, not experience.

The rules were now specific to the two of them, not what was laid out on the wall. She'd pulled the leash from his hands, so it was up to her to give it back to him and accept his punishment. If that was what she wanted.

She'd broken out in a sweat, holding that tether in clammy palms. When she made the first step, she had to stop and steady her wobbling knees. But in his home, even at the Adlers', she could feel him, separate from everyone else. If she could calm down, and focus, she somehow knew she could feel him, find him. He was watching her intently; she was sure of it. He'd promised to be no farther away than ten feet. He wouldn't break his word. He just wouldn't give in to her fear. Everyone else had, all these months, but he was ruthless, ruthless as only the Master of her dreams could be. He believed the submissive in her was stronger than the wounded creature she thought she'd become. He wouldn't abandon her, but he would force her to trust that he was there, to find him and hand him the leash again.

She wanted to trust him that way, but she hadn't let herself face the fear that came with increased dependency. She'd hidden in her room, let her ability to trust get as weak and flaccid as her muscles. Taking one step forward was harder than anything she'd ever done. Her heart rate accelerated. She had no idea what was in front of her. She should crouch down, go to hands and knees to feel her way along the floor like a groveling animal. But Gram would be appalled, clucking about hygiene, hundreds of feet that had been God knew where, traipsing across the carpet.

A half laugh, half sob choked out of her. As if that mattered right now. The pulse of the music drummed through her feet, loud enough that she could hear the song and words. Sade. "Nothing Can Come Between Us." It had been one of her favorites. It *was* one of her favorites. Taking a step, she breathed. One step, one breath. She could have been any sub whose Master had blindfolded her beneath her mask, a sensory deprivation to increase the intensity of the experience.

Intense was definitely the right word. She took another step, and brushed cloth.

A suit jacket. Her knuckles grazed a shirt's small, smooth buttons, then moved to a lapel. It wasn't Peter. She'd known that as soon as she came within range, because she knew his scent, his heat. But this man wasn't unfamiliar. Jon. Sage, a smell she'd associated with him, mixed with the whiskey he'd been drinking. When he'd asked her what drink she'd like, he'd taken her hand in an easy motion, pressed her knuckles to his chest, so she recognized the texture of the jacket. He passed his own knuckles over her cheek now, below the mask, and grazed her lips with...chocolate?

Chocolate and brandy, a cordial. When she parted her lips, he placed it on her tongue, caressing her throat as she took it. While she was occupied with savoring the unique, rich taste, he let her feel that he was holding something soft, almost like a clay, in his other hand. It had a form to it, as though there were wires beneath the malleable substance. He leaned in, his mouth against her ear.

"Peter's demand. I'm going to put these two things on you, dearest. Draw a breath in, so I have a little room. He's got you laced quite tight, the sadist."

That voice was pitched exactly as she'd suspected. Despite his tone of gentle amusement, Jon was quite capable of issuing a command as a Master. Whatever bound these men together, it made it impossible for her to feel threatened by him now.

Peter had reminded her in the car that she'd been a submissive for as long as she could remember. The relief that could come from obedience to a man she knew could handle her, that she could trust and test by turns, was an elusive but familiar shadow she wanted to chase down, pull into herself and leave fear behind. *Peter's demand...*

Holding still, she took a breath, the chocolate melting on her tongue. Jon's long, clever fingers slid into the corset, worked across to her nipples and then pinched that disk of clay over each. He had a sensual touch, functional and caressing at once, so that the pressure made her catch his sleeves, steadying herself at the rocket of sensation. Then his hands slid free, resting on her shoulders. It was like Play-Doh. Her lips curved at the ridiculous thought; then something began to happen that drove away any thought of a child's toy. It was warming. Warming, and something else. It penetrated her nerve endings and... Holy God, her nipples were getting terribly aroused, as if Peter were suckling them, tugging, creating a liquid pool in her lower belly that had her off balance.

While her body shuddered, Jon turned her, sending her from him with a gentle nudge. With fear being supplanted by physical desire, she dared a few more steps, wondering if he'd sent her toward Peter.

Instead, she stumbled over her shoes, but someone caught her from behind as she gasped. Ben. He was easy, so larger-than-life sexy, his aftershave a rich, teasing scent.

"Need to get you back in those shoes to protect your feet, darling."

...you can touch or explore anything within your range...

It was too much to resist. Rather than complying, she reached back, found the knot of his silky tie, and threaded it through her fingers. His hands closed on her hips, steadying her. She arched, her tongue teasing her own lips at the additional stimulation to her nipples. The movement brought her ass fully against his groin, and holy God. Talk about a portfolio. Ben had gotten extra blessings from the cock fairy. She couldn't help it, not with that stimulation happening to her nipples. Thinking about Peter watching, remembering their lap dance, she made a slow, sensual circle, her lips curving at an expulsion of air on her nape that suggested she'd inspired a half chuckle, or a muttered curse. Ben tightened his fingers, made her step into those shoes.

"You're trouble, darling. That's for sure. Go on with you, now." Since she'd let Ben's tie drape over her shoulder, the silk passed over the high top of her breast as she moved away. This time she attempted that pendulum saunter, biting her lips at the sensations that sparked through her nipples like electricity. Straight ahead she went, not at all surprised to come up against Lucas.

This was why she could move ten feet however she wanted. Peter's friends had formed a loose circle around her. How they were doing it in a crowded club environment, she had no idea, but she was learning not to question the miracles Peter could pull off. She wouldn't run into anything, touch anything Peter knew she shouldn't. Of course, he might have something to say about that little tease she'd given Ben, but if he reacted the way he had in the car, she'd go back and give Ben a full lap dance to experience that punishment again.

But now there was Lucas. Broad shoulders, tight, athletic body. An amateur cyclist, according to the earlier small talk. Intriguing choice, all of them wearing suits or more formal attire. His shirt was probably some impressive brand like Armani, with that soft, feel-me texture, though the chest beneath had its own appeal. His hands were holding her firmly under her elbows, a Master's hands. His knee brushed against her bare leg, making her hyperaware of how easy it would be for him to shift, widen her stance so he could press a bicycle-hard thigh between her legs. His lips were against her ear now, though, feeding her eagerness to have more pleasures woven into her lust-fogged mind.

"We all have our specialties, sweet Dana. If Ben had his way with you, he'd take you in the ass, keep you screaming and climaxing at once. Jon has his many clever devices, and my specialty..." He took her hand to his mouth, and enclosed two fingers there, making her gasp at the artful way his tongue swept between the knuckles, such an obvious representation of the way he might penetrate a woman's pussy that her pulse sped up when he let them slide slowly out and then took them down to her panties. He pressed her fingers over her soaked thong. "Those might be my lips there, if Peter allows us the pleasure and opportunity at some future time. But tonight is just for you to feel the possibilities."

Holy crap, her knees were weak. If Peter willed it, these men might do even more, bring her pleasure in multiple ways at once. She wondered if they'd ever shared Cassandra or Savannah, if those women craved such extreme play the way she had. The way she *did*. An erotic shiver went through her at the certainty of it.

When Lucas let her go, he didn't nudge her in a specific direction as the others had. He simply stepped back, letting her decide where she would go. She'd wrapped the leash around one arm to keep from tripping on it, but she'd preferred it taut, one end in Peter's hand. Her anger had dissipated. She was anxious, aroused, her mind spinning, but she moved forward without fear now, convinced they wouldn't allow any missteps. As such, the next obstacle surprised her, because it wasn't male. Or a familiar body.

She'd walked into an occupied St. Andrews' cross. Exploring, Dana found lovely, thick hair that tumbled down soft shoulders. She drew back when she brushed what was obviously a bare breast. A female slave. If she was in the public area, her Master or Mistress was likely encouraging a limited amount of touching. No one had stopped her yet, so cautiously, Dana reached out again, investigated a pair of breasts far heavier and fuller than her own. Aroused nipples, despite the raised welts on the generous curves. A hardcore pain slave. Despite that, in sympathy, she bent, kissed the abraded flesh. The woman quivered beneath her mouth.

Dana couldn't hear her reaction, which meant either it was below her hearing threshold or, more likely, she was gagged. The shudder was pleasure, though, so she continued to investigate, finding the restrained submissive had a curved belly and Venus's thighs to match the breasts. A voluptuous woman. She liked that, liked the woman's smooth skin. She bit back a helpless little moan of her own as the strobing feel of whatever Jon had put on her nipples increased, responding to her own elevating arousal. She pinched this woman's nipples, a reflection of how much she wanted her own teased. She thought of what Peter had said about the breast bondage, imagined it in detail. She wanted that. She wanted Peter.

What she was doing must be pleasing him, so she decided to push it further, see how much he could take before he got involved. Coming closer to the woman, she ran her hands over the curvy body, learning her, grazing her knuckles over a puffy clit. The restrained slave hadn't come yet, or had been built back up to mindless heights again. Dana pressed her corseted breasts against the woman's and whimpered at the sensation against her stiff nipples. She rubbed herself there, trying to get relief, even as she found the woman's stretched mouth with her fingertips and kissed her over the ball gag, kissing her like she wanted Peter to kiss her. Hard, demanding.

She rubbed her silk-clad pussy against one of those pillowy thighs, across the woman's mound, and clung to the posts above her as the woman cried out. Rotating her hips and then thrusting forward, Dana brought pressure and friction against the woman's mound. From the back she knew it looked as though she was fucking the woman as a man would, all the while giving them a generous display of her ass.

Was the blindness making her abandon all inhibitions, or was it the overstimulation of her nipples, the feast to the senses his men had just given her? She didn't know, but she was yearning toward what all subs sought, that subspace where rational thinking meant nothing and responding to one's Master was everything, giving pleasure and receiving it.

Peter was a breast man. Turning, she leaned back against the woman's body and plucked at the front of her own corset, unhooking the top several eyelets, then cupped her breasts, displaying them. When her nipples, encased in Jon's diabolical creation, brushed the top edge, she bit back a cry at the near-climactic sensation, arching back into the woman. Oh, God, if her Master or Mistress freed her hands, but not her legs, that woman could cinch an arm around Dana's waist, reach around to Dana's pussy, bring her to climax while the men watched, growing harder and harder.

She liked the idea, felt the power of it, desire and lust pulsing toward her. She wondered how much of an audience she had. Now she felt no fear of it, because she knew that protected circle was around her. What were Cassandra and Savannah doing? Were they watching, or doing similar things? Or did these Dominants bring their women here for arousal and voyeurism only, confining their play to more semi-private methods? Was that another reason this circle of men were around her? The message being that she was here to serve Peter's pleasure, but not available to others except someone like this restrained slave, who'd become another enhancement to their private pleasures?

When they'd wanted to touch her, with Peter's consent, it had only been more stimulating, fuel thrown on the fire. It was all about her pleasure, as he'd said. She didn't feel handicapped or pitiful. She felt cared for, not as someone who needed protection, but as someone who'd been given it because they didn't want to share. The idea swept her with feminine power. But she also burned with a craving want, and that want had a specific target. She'd wanted him to come to her.

But he was her Master. She'd pulled the leash from *his* hand. Sliding away from the woman, she stopped, trying to concentrate past her arousal. It wasn't only their intoxicating combinations of male scents that told her they were close to her. She could detect body heat, some kind of pulsing...energy. For the first time in nearly a year, she didn't notice that she couldn't see or hear. Her other senses were giving her so much, she could see them around her in every way that mattered. She felt the hold of the corset keenly, the power it gave her through its possession, and responded to it. Lifting her head, she straightened her shoulders further. Using her heart and soul, she found the unique signature, the male scent she wanted, the one for whom she wore the corset. Adjusting her direction, she walked six steps, and knelt, bowing her head and holding up the leash. "Forgive me, Master."

It was noisy, but not that noisy. He heard her. Peter stared down at her bowed head, the offered leash. She'd driven them all crazy with that performance. Hard as a rock, he was raging to put his claim on her. Lucas, Jon and Ben had all done what came naturally to them, and Peter had been satisfied with how it increased her desire. These men were capable of giving any woman the most intense orgasms of her life. He'd love to give her that gift...another night. She hadn't been his long enough, and there was still too much ground to cover, before he would be willing to share more than this.

He'd had a bad moment when she jerked the leash away. He'd known she was more hardcore, but that had been before. Afraid he'd gone too far, something in him had broken loose. Fuck, he didn't care what the right thing was to do. He was going to do what he'd wanted from the first. Scoop her up, take her away, protect her from every- thing. He couldn't stand doing this to her, seeing her fear and pain.

It had been Jon who'd steadied him, placing a hand on his arm, giving him a calming look before he stepped out and let Dana run into him first. And now, in those six steps she'd taken toward him, Dana had given *herself* a glimpse of what she could choose for herself. Maybe it would lead her to trusting him, not just for this scenario, but to the deepest levels of her soul, so eventually she might choose him. Then he could spend his life ensuring she never regretted that choice.

Taking the leash from her hand, he wrapped it around her wrists, holding on to them for a few long moments, tracing the fragile bone and smooth skin. When he at last drew her to her feet, he brought her to him, keeping the leash taut this time. The bare brush of her body against him, the near embrace, the tremble that swept through her as a result, almost broke him. But with a light squeeze of her hands, he guided her through the circle of the other K&A men, to the opposite wall where a favorite device waited.

The advantage to this kind of private club was that sex was allowed in the "public" areas. He was ready as hell to take advantage of that perk. At this point, it wasn't a perk—it was a damn necessity.

Guiding her hands to it, he let her explore the breast stock while he released the sliding adjustment. As he found the right size, her fingers drifted down his back, grazing his arms. Most Masters had firm rules about their subs touching them without permission, but he liked how she used him as an anchor in unfamiliar surroundings. He couldn't get enough of it. But eventually he turned her square to him and opened up the hooks of her corset until it gapped below her breasts. When he removed Jon's invention, he bit back a groan, seeing how distended the nipples were. The boning of the corset was stiff, but he was able to fold it back enough that he could guide her breasts into the two spaced circles in the smooth mahogany wood. Tightening the metal adjustments inside the circles diminished their size, so that it held her fast. Her blood vessels would constrict, enlarging her breasts and making them more sensitive.

He raised the height of the stock, so she was straining on her toes. Then he placed the nipple clamps on her. She cried out at the stimulation, biting her lip at the pain that came with it. Easing the screws, he found that balance where she was on the knife-edge, her tremor from intense arousal, not unbearable pain. Then he connected the clamps with a chain, meeting in the middle with a padlock he held in his palm. Guiding her bound hands up to feel where he'd placed her, he saw her register how the stock worked, like one of old, only instead of arms, its torturous focus was on a woman's luscious curves. The circle adjustments kept her there with a snug hold, but as an added psychological measure, the locked chain between the nipple clamps underscored how impossible it was for her to pull away and free herself.

When he let the padlock fall out of his hand, she jerked hard, a cry wrenching from her throat at the shock of the sudden pull against the clamps and her already hugely aroused nipples. Beautiful, mauve, impossibly aroused peaks.

"Oh, God, Master..."

She was so wet that her thighs glistened with it, the thong useless to absorb her arousal. He loved it, couldn't wait to strip her out of it and take her in only the stockings, corset and collar. If he had his way, that was what he'd always have her wear when she was in his house, in his bed.

"Now for what I promised you." He made the words wet, covering her ear with his lips, dipping in with his tongue to trace the crevices around her hearing aid. "I'm going to make you come by sucking your pretty tits, sweetheart. You're going to gush like a man. I know you want my cock, but you'll wait for that, as punishment for pulling the leash out of my hands, until you'll never do that again, will you?"

She shook her head wildly, eyes glazed and mouth parted. "Please... Master."

Jon had had a staff person bring Peter a chair, so now he sat to study the display in front of him, stretching out his legs under the stock so they pressed against her calves on either side. She shifted on her toes, making the muscles in her thighs and that heart-shaped ass strain. Her gorgeous tits looked round and heavy. The lock was dragging her bare nipples down, which he knew were tingling like a son of a bitch. Taking his time, he leaned forward and blew on one.

She screamed, convulsed in aroused reaction. He wanted to do this forever, but because he didn't want to damage those tender blood vessels with prolonged constriction, he closed in, put his mouth over one nipple and the clamp.

"Oh, God, oh, God..." It was a chant. On another night, he'd ask Lucas to lick the fluids trickling down her leg, all the way back up to her cunt, start drinking that nectar he liked so much, while Ben slid a few nicely lubricated things in and out of her pretty little puckered anus. She'd come again and again, until she was so exhausted they'd have to carry her. But tonight, he wanted her to come from his mouth on her nipples only, a reminder that he could command her response. That he could take care of her in all ways.

Oh, fuck, she tasted like butterscotch. Jon thought of everything. He suckled her, so gently, because hard would have been way too much right now. It was the thing he'd learned first about pleasuring a woman, and it remained the most important. Take it slow and easy, keep it slow and easy, until she was begging mindlessly for it rough, and then the time was right to let loose his own needs. That was fine; he was so hard, he wasn't getting out of the chair until the very second he intended to ram his cock into her.

Her head thrashed this way and that, fighting her restraint not because she wanted to be freed, but because her body had to move in response to the stimulus. He moved to the other nipple, teasing that one, swirling, nipping, then slow, long drags of his tongue. He brought his hands into it, adding to the squeezing sensation, milking her breasts into his mouth while she became animal and savage, her words reflecting the fact he'd put his claim on a soldier as well as a good churchgoing girl.

"Oh...fuck. Please fuck me.... Let me fucking come. Oh, God... love you sucking my tits... Please, Master... My cunt needs you."

He kept sucking, licking, biting. Her legs were shaking, but he didn't need to worry about her falling against the restraint and hurting herself. Ben materialized out of the shadows and slid a capable arm around her waist, holding her steady. He met Peter's eyes, gave him a nod, and Peter kept doing his magic on her breasts. Ben had to be light on his toes, because in her state, her pussy was seeking his hard thigh to rub and hump. He kept his leg away from what was Peter's alone tonight as a flush rose along her throat and the expanse of smooth flesh above his mouth. Her face was straining, lips pulled back in a pre-orgasmic snarl. Peter bit, sucked harder now, and squeezed one last time, pushing her over.

Her shrieks could have been heard in the lobby, as if he hadn't already attracted a sizable crowd. He and the other K&A men weren't normally public players. Cassandra and Savannah were sitting up in a mezzanine seat with Matt, where they had a good view of the display, but were not part of it. Peter liked keeping his woman to himself as well, but he'd known Dana needed the more hardcore, the sensory overload. It would push her into the mindless ecstasy state that was a Master's drug, where nothing stood in the way of her true self and desires.

As her climax rocked her against the stock, her hips pumped wildly. Ben was intent on her reaction, his jaw tight and eyes green fire. Some girl was going to get the ass-fucking of her life tonight. A submissive who could handle his rougher needs. Probably more than one.

Peter rose, circled around. Ben held her until Peter opened his slacks, slid a condom on, and then the lawyer stepped out of the way. Perfectly in sync, Peter's arm slid around her waist as Ben's was sliding away. As she collapsed back against Peter, he slammed into her cunt, into rippling, slick-as-an-ocean flesh. She was still coming, her pussy oozing sweet honey as he plunged into it.

She cried out again, an animal cry of satisfaction. Digging his fingers under the collar, he grasped her throat, protected it from dangerous pressure as he held her head up, drawing the tether taut between its hold on the D-ring and her hands as he worked his hips against her ass, striving for deeper.

"Fuck..." He came as violently, ramming her so her tits pressed harder through those holes, the lock swinging in a way that had her flinching even through her pleasure. Jon moved into Peter's chair, grasping the lock so it couldn't cause her further pain. As she whimpered through aftershocks and Peter's final thrusts, Jon removed it, as well as the nipple clamps. Knowing the blood surge could be intense, he brought his fingers into play, massaging her sore breasts as he loosened the stock. She moaned at the additional stimulation, but stayed where she was, good little slave that she was.

Peter shuddered with her through their aftermath, even though he wanted to be where Jon was, making sure she didn't experience the terrible pain that could sometimes come with the returning blood flow. Damn, he wanted to be everywhere at once. Jon gave him a wry smile, backing off as Peter's hands came around and took over, earning another dove's cry of need from his sweet girl. She was near full collapse; he could feel it. There was nothing medically wrong with her, no, but the workout this morning had told him what her conditioning was, where her limits were. He had promised he'd always take care of her, and he wasn't going to fall down on the job.

Glancing up at the viewing mezzanine, he saw there was no space between Matt and Savannah and Cassandra, the women sitting on either side of him. Though of course Cassandra was all Lucas's, that odd code that bound them permitted some liberties in such an arousing environment. So Cassandra leaned into Matt's support, her fingers working up and down his thigh in a needy little gesture while Matt had his hand discreetly up Savannah's tight skirt, probably fingering her beautiful pussy in slow circles. Her lips were already parted, her throat working. He had his other arm around Cassandra's shoulders, fingers lightly running up and down her upper arm. His knuckles grazed the side of her breast, which displayed a very attractively jutting nipple through the hold of her snug knit dress, since Lucas had had her shed the bra in the shadows of the limo.

As Peter expected, Lucas appeared beside them. Cass was up and in his arms, nearly climbing up his body such that he hitched her up, let her wind her legs around him as he cupped her ass and took her away toward a private room. Matt and Savannah rose, Matt supporting Savannah around the waist as they followed. They'd been known to take the same room, and enjoy the pleasure of watching one another, though they didn't often invite the single members of the group to such displays. That was all right. Jon and Ben were already seeking their own partners, seeing Peter had things well in hand, literally.

He was now alone with his remarkable woman, trembling with reactions as strong as what he himself was feeling. Removing his condom, he eased her back from the stock. Before he could arrange his clothes and lift her in his arms, she'd turned and dropped to her knees. With hardly a hesitation, she found him, closed her mouth around his drained cock, licking and cleaning him, a desperate grati- tude that pierced his heart as he saw the tears. Withdrawing gently, he fastened his slacks and bent, lifting her. She nestled into him, her wrists still bound, else he suspected she would have wrapped herself around his shoulders.

He wasn't going to one of the rooms, he realized. He was taking her home. He wanted to be with her at home.

CHAPTER TWELVE

*T*he limo would return for the others. Peter had told her that, but said little else. It wasn't an awkward silence. She didn't say anything, because she couldn't speak. She'd never had an orgasm like that—hell, an experience—in her life. She'd shuddered and jerked for a good half hour now, so that Peter had moved her into his lap, holding her close, pressing kisses into her brow and murmuring to her. Her nipples were still vibrating, and occasionally he would touch them, stroke and massage in a way that kept a low simmer of arousal swirling.

"I don't understand," she said at last. She could hear the broken tone in her voice, echoing in her head, knew it reflected what was shattering inside her.

"What?" He tipped up her chin, traced her cheek, telling her he was looking into her face. He'd removed the mask, but now his hand passed over where it had pressed into her skin, reminding her of it. Her tears fell without her permission all the time, so why she ducked her head now, embarrassed, she didn't know. But he kept her face up. "Tell me, sweetheart. Don't cry. Your tears will destroy me."

She heard it again, that mysterious dark lake of his emotions that kept reaching toward her and then withdrawing before she could grasp it. She gripped his wrist. "It's too intense. I know it's not just sex between us, Peter. But how can I... I can't wrap my mind around this in a couple days, make any kind of decision about anything. I'm terrified to rely on you, to be disappointed, or to disappoint you. I mean, hell, if I'd come back whole and we'd dated, I would have been in a position of strength. Not needy and dependent. How do I know you know what you're getting into? How do I know any of this is real, for either of us?"

He was silent for a bit, silent enough to make her worry, to make her wish she'd said nothing. See, she was already too clingy. God, what had happened to the woman who'd plunged into a firefight?

"First," he said at last, "I completely agree. There's no way you can make a decision about us in two days. I never expected you to do that. What I want is for you to decide that we're worth a shot, and stay with me. See how it goes."

"I don't want you paying for stuff and—"

"Then we make a damn budget and cut it down the middle. If you want to eventually get your own place nearby, to prove something to yourself, fine." The spark of temper was oddly reassuring. "That's not what this is about and you know it. What if you *had* come back healthy and whole? Do you think you'd want me any less? Do you think I'd want you any less than I do now? How did you feel about me before that bomb exploded, Dana? Tell me."

She wanted to resist him, but she couldn't fight her own honesty. "I couldn't wait to see you again." The unconscious word choice formed a lump in her throat. "I dreamed of you. Wanted you so much it hurt."

His fingers slid over the ache, caressing the throat bound in his collar. "You do see me, Dana. And I see the woman I met a year ago. The woman I still want, the woman I can't wait to discover more about every day."

She blinked back tears. "How do I know you aren't staying with me out of pity? I do know you, Peter. You're honor bound to save the damsel in distress. You don't know anything else."

"I'm honor bound to stand by the woman I love," he responded. When a little sob escaped her, he traced her tears, kissed them away. Dana had to hold on to him, so hard her nails dug through his shirt. Maybe she imagined it, but the voice that spoke against her ear had a suspicious break to it. "I'm only scared shitless that you might not want to stay. I've never held a woman against her will."

"Oh, really?" she managed. "What do you call being forced out of your house and flown off in the middle of the night? You have a problem with 'no means no,' Captain."

He gave a shaky half laugh. "Don't change the subject. You're so worried about what's happening in *my* head. How do I know you aren't staying with me out of some weak-assed dependency?"

She swatted at him. "Peter Winston. I haven't said I'm doing *anything* yet."

"If we trust each other, we'll both know the truth in time. We'll know it's love, real and true." Guiding her now-captured hand to his jaw, he let her feel the resolve in his mouth, touch his lips, so she couldn't mistake his meaning. "In the long run, the doubts won't matter, Dana. You're going to become more self-reliant every day, and one day you'll know for sure why you're with me. I know how important that is. You'll start giving me shit about being overprotective, and I'll shout back. We'll fight, make up, the way couples do. But you'll always admit I'm right, because you want me to be happy."

It startled a snort out of her. "I wouldn't count on that one, Captain."

He shifted beneath her, tightened his arms. "You've lost your sight, some of your hearing. You haven't lost your brain, your sense of touch, smell, your inner strength. Your soul." His fingers touched the Lord's Hands, sliding along her shoulder blade. "Every time a soldier goes into battle, he's believing in something more than his physical body. Whether he calls it God, luck or his own damn gut, he does. The body's a crutch."

He put her hand on his heart, and did the same with his own, the heel pressed to the high curve of her breast. "This is the real deal, what we all rely on when everything else is taken away. Tonight, for a few precious seconds, you knew that. I saw it in the way you held yourself, the way you walked to me and handed me that leash back, regal as a princess."

Because of him. His refusal to let her hide from herself, his willingness to use his friends and all their seductive talents, as well as his own, to tap into the deepest part of herself, a part that wasn't destroyed by that bomb. A path to re-creating the rest. And he was asking her to rely on his heart while she took that journey.

Closing her eyes, she pressed her lips together. "Peter...my family is gone. Gram died I guess the way a person's supposed to go, but my parents, my brothers... They were taken, in a way. I've never considered myself damaged, just good at getting along and doing what needs to be done. But you're offering your heart to me. Even if I could look past any worries I have about whether or not that's real, I've got a terrible fear about that."

Despite her best attempt, her voice broke. She tried to steady it, trying not to fall apart, but here were the damn tears again. "That fear says, 'How much more do I have to lose? How much more can I take?' I feel all alone, anticipating the day you'll be gone, like everyone else."

"Damn it, you're not alone." He tucked her head underneath his chin, his arms becoming steel bands, every muscle hard and sure against her. "I knew you for one night, went off to damn Afghanistan for a year and couldn't shake you. Your scent, your voice, everything you are. I'm willing to take the chance that fate knows something I don't, that it's going to give us a long time together, time to make this thing we've got deeper, harder and more powerful and peaceful than we can imagine. So that if we do lose one another to something in the future, even if it's old age, we'll know every second was worth it."

He lifted her up, so she felt his gaze on her face again. "As for how much you have to take, you have to take it all. Every bit of love and life you're given. I bet that's what your Gram taught you."

She thought of that, all the way home.

Home. When he opened the door, guided her through it, Dana took a couple steps, stopped and breathed it in. His home, one he wanted to share with her. One he wanted her to be a part of, to make it theirs.

Thinking about that, she moved forward, using her fingertips to find her way, drifting along the easy chair with the stuffed kitten, the side table, the table with the vase and chess set. She already knew more about where everything was here than she had in the place she'd stayed for months. As if she *wanted* to know this place. Or already knew it, somehow. Just as she seemed to know him. He moved behind her, slow. He was keeping pace with her, but remaining silent, as if he understood she was debating something important.

She felt his tension, that murky undercurrent she'd felt off and on from the first moment he'd darkened her door again. Those were the emotions that would tell her what he was truly thinking and feeling. Would he give her those if she asked, or did he think she couldn't handle whatever they were? And was he right?

But he kept following her. Slow steps. Each time she stopped, he did as well, always a little closer to her, closing that distance, ratcheting up that tension. Her pulse elevated with the increase in heat, from him or her, she couldn't tell. When she reached his bedroom, she turned at the foot of his bed. He hadn't put the dress back on her, but he'd wrapped her in his suit coat. The hem of it brushed her thighs. Letting the jacket slip off her shoulders, she stepped out of her shoes. Then, after a brief hesitation, she turned her back to him and removed the thong, then the stockings, a slow slide of silk down quivering thighs.

He'd given her a safe word. Freedom. The implications of the word hit her, the word he'd chosen so randomly a lifetime ago.

Under his restraint, she'd soared higher that night at The Zone than she ever had in her life. Until tonight. Or the next time they came together in this desperate-tender-rough-everything way they seemed to have.

She left the corset and collar on. They gave her the confidence to make a frightening choice, to say the word aloud.

"Peter." She knew she'd whispered, because she couldn't hear it, but the name echoed in her heart.

"I'm here, sweetheart." He was, right in front of her, and she reached up, cupped his face. Not as Master and slave in this moment, though it was there, a deep bond between them.

"You said, if I decided to stay, accepted that I was yours...you would make love to me in your bed."

His hand was over his, gripping hard. "I meant it."

"So do I." She hesitated as he pressed a kiss to her palm, her body already shuddering, anticipating the pleasure they'd bring each other. "I'm scared. I'll probably stay scared and mad for a while. I want to trust you, but it will all take time, won't it?"

"Yeah." He slid his arms around her, hitched her up so her legs could curl around his hips, feel the arousal he pressed between her thighs. "A really, really long time."

Her lips curved. "I don't think we're talking about the same thing, Captain."

"Yeah, we are, Sergeant. It all means the same. And I know how much you love wearing these"—his hand swept down the corset, came back to rest on the collar—"but for this, I want it to be skin to skin. I want you to know if it's all stripped away, nothing but us, that I'll be there for you, with you."

She swallowed. Nodded. Then halted him by holding his hands for a minute. "Skin to skin, Peter. Please give me everything. Don't be afraid I can't take it. Stop holding back your emotions from me. I need to know I'm not made of glass. I need everything you are, too."

His fingers gripped her harder, and she held her breath. "I'll try," he said at last.

Then he was putting her back on her feet so he could unhook the foundation garment. The sensation of being unwrapped, unbound by him, was as arousing as being laced into it. His hands made all the difference. Releasing the collar, he let it all fall away. With his palms he soothed the lines the tight fit of the corset had left. Then he lifted her again, carried her around to the side of the bed and laid her down, stroking her face before he came down and covered her lips with his.

He was such a big man. She liked that, liked the aura of heat around him, liked the fact he didn't mind when she reached up and traced where their lips joined. He kept kissing her as she explored his face, the curl of lashes, the lines across his forehead and around his eyes, his strong facial structure. Short, silken hair, just as she remembered.

Moving down to her breasts, he nursed the sore tips, aroused and soothed at once, until she was quivering, her hips rising to signal what she needed. His palm slid along her thigh, teased her mound, but then he capitulated to the tug of her hands and lay down upon her, chest to thigh, letting her feel all of him. He'd stripped, so they were blissfully naked in each other's arms. The curve of muscle along his back, the breadth of his shoulders and network of bone and muscle were there, accessible to her touch. The different texture of skin where she remembered the *PEACE* tattoo followed his shoulders, the *Don't Tread On Me* flag against his impressive biceps. She traced the letters where she imagined them to be. P...E...A...C...E.

Her body was spinning slowly toward a climax, as strong and pleasurable as at the club, but so soft and easy at once. This was what peace was. The pleasure and time to do this, wrapped in a cocoon of darkness that was comforting, not frightening, because every chamber of her mind, her heart and her soul was filled with him.

He was hard and ready for her. When he slid in, she tilted up to meet him, an instinct as old as life itself, two coming together to be one. It brought a guttural sigh of pleasure from her lips and he made a similar noise against her ear. Fondling her neck, he followed the line of the hearing aid and stroked the shell of her ear. "Am I too heavy?" His voice was throaty, thick.

She shook her head, wrapping her arms around his shoulders and breathing him in, pressing her face into his corded neck. Her heels slid over his taut buttocks, the rhythmic press and release, the matching sensation in her womb as he slid in, slid out, his movements powerful, but slow, cherishing. As he'd said, a natural skin-to-skin meeting, the need to be inside each other taking over everything else.

He curved his powerful back in order to cup her breasts together again, which loosened her hold but made her arch into his mouth as he nursed on them. His tongue flicked over her flesh, at first with gentle playfulness, but then a more insistent lashing. She thought of what he'd said, about having them pierced, and thought she would like that, knowing he would adorn them as he wished, and tease her into mindless arousal like this.

He was putting more thrust into his strokes, and her body was responding, rising like an opposing wave to meet that impact.

"Oh, God..." She clasped his broad shoulders, the sensations becoming too much. She loved his mouth, his beautiful cock, all of him. Everything about him. All hers, hers, hers...

She clutched him with her muscles, wanting him to come, wanting to feel it, and realized he hadn't put on a condom on. That bareback sensation she'd wanted was there now, and while she knew the risk was minimal this time of the month, it was all right. She just knew it was.

"I needed to feel you," he said hoarsely against her ear. "I'm sorry."

She shook her head, tears springing to her eyes again. *When it's the right one, you hear each other's thoughts, know his mind like your own.* Gram, talking about Granddad, her eyes full of distant, misty love and memory.

In answer, she held him tighter, inside and out. He increased the power of his thrusts and she met him, the sensations inundating her such that she thought she'd probably never experienced the act as deeply or intensely, physically or emotionally.

"Peter... Master... I'm so close. Please..."

"Come for me."

She shattered in his arms, like plunging into waves of warm tropical waters, churned in a wild direction as the surf caught her up, headed toward shore, toward home. She cried out, and that cry intensified as his joined her, his seed releasing in a hot, searing rush that drove her higher, gave her climax an extra jolt of intensity that kept her clinging to him, working her hips up against his, her legs clamped tight around him.

As he came down, she realized he was breathing hard, harder than a fit man should, even after a climax. When she reached up to his face, he caught her fingers, but she lifted the other hand, refusing to be dissuaded.

"Peter, you promised. All of you, too, remember?"

He made a noise of protest, but he couldn't grab both her hands because his other arm was holding his full weight off her. When her fingers rested lightly on his cheeks, felt the dampness of something that wasn't sweat, her brow furrowed. "Peter."

"You're beautiful, Dana. You're everything I want. And I almost lost you before I found you. It's tearing me up inside, not letting you see how crazy it's made me. I love you. I'm sorry if you can't handle hearing that, or you don't believe it. But I do."

Raw, quiet words, uttered in a rough voice that tore into her worse than shrapnel. But it was the missing piece. She'd been right to ask for all of it, to find the bravery to face it. With their emotions twining around them, binding them even closer, she was finally ready to hear anything he needed to share. Closing her eyes, she held him tighter. She'd needed to hear the voice of his soul, as raw and fragile as her own. For months he'd written her letters, without her writing back. He'd come to her, brought her here, bullied and cajoled.

Loved her.

There was nothing else to call it, no matter what skeptics said, those who relied on some irrational formula between emotion and the passage of time. In truth, those letters had been her lifeline, helping her to hold on until he got to her. Which meant she very likely loved him as much, right back.

When she'd stood at his bed, and told him she wanted him to make love to her, that she would stay, she hadn't really understood *why* she would stay. She'd still feared it might be lack of options, or something else equally destructive. But that moment had been too overwhelming, his body too close behind her, his powerful need, and she'd gone forward on faith or mindless instinct. Now she knew it wasn't anything destructive. No matter what had happened in Iraq, he was right. This would have happened between them, because something stronger than sex had forged their bond that night at The Zone.

She brought her hands back to his face, cupped his jaw. He was so powerful, so strong. Yet the heart was both the strongest and most fragile part of any person. Her Gram had told her that, too. She'd said, "If you find someone strong enough to love you through thick and thin, you don't never take that for granted, girl. Because if he loves you that much, that means you're the person who can break his heart."

"I'm so, so sorry, Peter," she said. More tears slid along her cheeks, found his fingers coming to collect them. "I'm sorry I didn't write you back. I'm sorry I made you be so strong, while I've been so lost. I want to be the type of person deserving of your love."

"Damn it, you already are."

"We both know there's a ways to go. I'm going to trust you to help me get there." She swallowed, took a deep breath and gave him a ghost of a smile. "But when I do, I'm going to learn to take care of you right back, Captain Winston. So you'd better watch out."

He pressed his forehead to hers. She heard the expulsion of his breath, and ran her hands up and down the broad back, slow, kneading, the strength of a river, the constancy of a woman's love, the promise of it in a touch. In some ways, it was the most intimate moment they'd yet shared.

"My mother warned me about short, determined women," he said at last, clearing his throat. "Said they're meaner than any other kind."

"Boy, you haven't seen anything," she whispered, catching the corner of his mouth with her own. When she tightened her arms around him, he did the same, nearly squeezing the breath out of her, his intense emotions washing through her, making her ache, happy, scared and anxious all at once. "You think I'm fragile, but I'm not."

"Yeah. You are in some ways." His hands gentled on her face. "I'm going to protect you, Dana. Love you. Always."

"Same as I'm going to do for you, Master."

~

Eventually, he lay next to her, making her smile anew since she knew he did it because he was worrying about his weight upon her, her considerate, loving Master. She was stronger than he believed. For the first time in a year, *she* believed it.

And instead of wishing this moment could stay the same, now she was thinking ahead, to other moments. Thinking of the next time he'd roll over and they'd do this all over again. What she'd do tomorrow. Where she'd go shopping with Cassandra and Savannah. What she'd do with her life. Peter would have her six. She could do anything she wanted, including care for him as well.

Her fingers drifted down his biceps, over that tattoo, bringing another thought. She didn't know how she felt about it, and she was afraid he would think she was asking because of her situation. No, she wouldn't bring it up now.

However, he had overly fine-tuned senses himself. He turned on his side, gathering her in to him, putting a thigh over hers, her breasts against the coarse hair of his chest. "What is it?"

She bit her lip. "Will you go overseas again?"

His arms constricted around her, his strength such that he was able to roll her halfway onto his body with the embrace. She snuggled into him, waiting for his answer.

"No. I'm going to resign my commission."

"What? Why?" She lifted her head. "Peter, I don't want you to make that decision because of me. I'll learn to take care of myself, and you shouldn't change your life. "

"You *have* changed my life, Dana." He put his lips to her temple, held them there. Tentatively she found his face, felt his closed eyes, the taut line of his jaw. "By taking care of you, I'm serving my country as well, in just as important a way."

"I'm not helpless."

"I know that. Tonight I took you into the most frightening thing a blind and deaf person can face. An entirely unfamiliar environment, lots of noise and challenges. You let it break you once, but then you put it together again. *You* did. In fact, you got pretty disobedient, playing with another slave for your own pleasure, taunting your Master and his friends. Rubbing yourself against Ben's monster dick."

He bent, nipped her throat, sharply enough she gasped, particularly when he slid his hand between her legs, reminding her of his right to touch her however, whenever he wished. Propping himself on an elbow, he touched her nose with a broad finger.

"Growing up, I had an old hound dog who was blind, deaf, and couldn't smell so well. He was fearless. Would run into things all the time, frustrating the hell out of him, but purely on an external level. He never let it get inside of him, make him stop being and doing what he wanted to be. He'd just get up and keep on going. You lost your confidence for a little bit. Never your courage."

"Are you calling me a bitch?" she demanded.

He brought her fingers to his mouth, let her feel his smile. "If the collar fits."

After a long pause, she spoke, a near whisper. "It does."

Looking down into her face, Peter saw her staring inward, as if she'd gone deep into herself, only this time maybe she'd found something worth seeing in the place where she still had her sight. Being here with her in this bed, making love to her, sharing his feelings with her, feeling her respond to him... There was nothing better. He didn't want her to be blind, but life could be everything they wanted it to be. This bond between them would make up for the lack of anything else. He was surer of it than ever before.

He couldn't wait for tomorrow, the next day. Hell, the next minute and hour, to watch their relationship grow, strengthen. Learn what irritated and pissed her off, get mad and make up, deal with the millions of big and little decisions that binding two lives together would bring. Hear her say "I love you" for the first time, without any worries. But for now, she gave him the next best thing.

She touched his face again, coming back to him, her smile soft, nervous. "I think...I think I love you, Peter Winston."

His heart flat broke open. His throat thickened in a way he was glad the other guys weren't around to see. Unable to speak, he found her other hand, guided it to her heart so she could feel what his fingers were doing beneath her own. He made that symbol, the one she'd pressed into his chest more than a year ago.

She'd given her heart to him then, and she'd surrendered it to him now. He was a soldier. Honor bound to take care of it, now and forever, he planned to do just that, with every beat of his own.

* * *

WANT MORE KNIGHTS OF THE BOARD ROOM? At forty-three, Rachel Madison yearns for a Master, but her confidence was destroyed by personal tragedy and an emotionally abusive ex-husband who didn't understand the gift of submission. Yet she keeps fantasizing about Jon Forte, the Kensington corporate executive who attends her yoga class. Though he's thirteen years younger than her, his Dominant nature only increases her longings.

When Jon notices her attention, he becomes determined to provide her everything she needs—in the way only the right Master can.

CLICK HERE TO READ NOW
AFTERLIFE

Reading this in print format?
Look for it at your favorite book vendor!

ABOUT THE AUTHOR

Having penned over fifty acclaimed BDSM contemporary and paranormal titles, which includes six award-winning series, *Joey W. Hill* has been awarded the RT Book Reviews Career Achievement Award for Erotic Romance. A submissive herself, Hill brings authenticity to her intensely emotional love stories.

She is grateful for the support of a wonderful and enthusiastic readership, which allows her to live on her beloved Carolina coast with her even more beloved husband and menagerie of animals.

- On the Web: https://storywitch.com
- Twitter: https://twitter.com/JoeyWHill
- Facebook: https://facebook.com/JoeyWHillAuthor
- Facebook Fan Forum: https://facebook.com/groups/ JWHMembersOnly
- MeWe: https://mewe.com/i/joeywhill
- GoodReads: https://www.goodreads.com/author/show/ 103359.Joey_W_Hill
- BookBub: https://bookbub.com/authors/joey-w-hill
- Amazon: https://amazon.com/Joey-W-Hill/e/B001JSCIW0

ALSO BY JOEY W. HILL

Mirror of My Soul

Mistress of Redemption

Rough Canvas

Branded Sanctuary

Divine Solace

Worth The Wait

Truly Helpless

In His Arms

Ignition Sequence

Naughty Bits Series

Naughty Bits

Naughty Wishes

Vampire Queen Series

Vampire Queen's Servant

Mark of the Vampire Queen

Vampire's Claim

Beloved Vampire

Vampire Mistress *(VQS: Club Atlantis)*

Vampire Trinity *(VQS: Club Atlantis)*

Vampire Instinct

Bound by the Vampire Queen

Taken by a Vampire

The Scientific Method

Nightfall

Elusive Hero

Night's Templar

Vampire's Soul

Vampire's Embrace

Vampire Master *(VQS: Club Atlantis)*

Vampire Guardian *(VQS: Club Atlantis)*

Vampire's Choice